Chesapeake Bay Christmas

Volume Four

The Bay Sisters

High Tide Publications, Inc.
1000 Bland Point Road
Deltaville, Virginia 23043
www.HighTidePublications.com

Ordering Information: Quantity sales. Special discounts are available on quantity purchases by corporations, associations, and others. For details, contact the "Special Sales Department" at the address above.

Editor:	Narielle Living
Cover:	Jeanne Johansen
Photography:	Julie Leverenz

Printed in the United States of America

Chesapeake Bay Christmas
Season Four
Diversity

We become not a melting pot, but a beautiful mosaic. Different People. Different Beliefs. Different Yearnings. Different Hopes. Different Dreams.

Jimmy Carter

This is the fourth year The Bay Sisters have written stories for the Christmas season, and this year (more than any other) the diversity of our individual lives shines through in the words on the pages in this book.

There is something for everyone this year — no matter your political, religious or spiritual leanings. Love is definitely the theme, but what kind of love?

To answer that question, you'll just have to read the book.

Table of Contents

THE LOVE BOAT

JM JOHANSEN

Chapter One

Colleen O'Brien Coffaro was a big woman. Rubenesque. Stout.

Colleen had not always been this way. In her youth, she took after her mother, a proud Irish woman who would tell you (any chance she got) that she could still fit into her wedding gown. "Fifty-six years ago, you know! I wore this gown when I was sixteen and I can still fit into it," she said as she slipped into it every year on her wedding anniversary and paraded through the living room in their apartment on the upper east side of New York.

Colleen would watch her mother's performance. She doubted she could get her left thigh into her own wedding dress. Colleen's size had increased exponentially with each year of her marriage to Antonio Coffaro. So now, after thirty-five years of marriage, she was well on her way to two hundred fifty pounds.

"I told you so. I knew you would get fat marrying that Iodálach. All that pasta and fat food, and three children to boot! I tried to talk you out of it, God knows. But you wouldn't listen. Now look at you."

"You know, Ma, he is the father of your grandchildren. Your only grandchildren, I might add. So I would knock it off if I were you."

"Or what," Ma retorted.

"Or nothing." Colleen knew when she was licked. "After all, if your only problem with me is my weight, I should thank God and all the saints that it stops there. After all, I can lose the weight, but you cannot lose your ignorance."

Her mother staggered back and fell against the sofa, grabbing her chest. "Colleen Margaret O'Brien, how dare you speak to your mother like that! Are you trying to kill me?"

Colleen said nothing, walked into the kitchen, and began to load the dishwasher with the dirty dishes from breakfast. Antonio had installed it for her last week. "It will make her life a little easier."

And only moments earlier Ma had called him an Iodálach.

Actually, Colleen was quite comfortable with her weight. True, when she married Antonio, she had weighed in at one hundred twenty pounds. "We got to get some meat on you," Antonio's mother had said before the wedding. She meant it, too, because every Sunday morning they would go to his mother's house after nine o'clock mass and help prepare the Sunday lunch. The red sauce (or gravy, as they called it) was started Saturday night so it would be ready in the morning. Right after mass, Mama C (as Colleen called Antonio's mother) would add whole Italian sausages made earlier in the week, pieces of beef, veal, lamb, and sometimes meatballs.

They didn't eat until two o'clock. There were appetizers to ward off hunger — prosciutto with melon, antipasto, Parmesan with grapes (or even jelly made from white wine).

At the dinner table, there would be bread, a huge pot of pasta, the meat cooked in the sauce in a separate dish to the side, and another small plate for salad. Then desert or coffee would be served after.

Ma had asked them to come for Sunday dinner. Antonio relented once, suffered the wrath of his mother, and they wound up going over later to Mama C's.

"How was it?" Mama C asked.

"First and last time," Antonio said.

And it was.

When Colleen would tell her husband about the conversations with her mother regarding her weight, he would laugh. "I love you just the way you are. Besides, you fit in with my family perfectly. Look at them. You, my love, are *È bionda, grassa e quarantenne.*"

Colleen laughed. "I'm not forty, you goose. I am fifty-six."

"You still are the twenty year old I married thirty-six years ago."

"And you, Antonio, are blind as a bat."

***

Colleen settled into the autumn cool with a strange sense of calm. After all, the hot summer was over, and it made it a much more pleasant climate for someone who found the New Jersey heat unbearable.

Christmas was upon them before she knew it. Her mother insisted on having Colleen's family over for Christmas Eve, where the children were allowed to open one present, taking the rest home for the morning ritual at Mama C's. Early in their marriage it had caused a problem with Mama C because Antonio's family celebrated the Feast of Seven Fishes on

Christmas Eve. "This is the tradition in our home," Colleen had told her mother-in-law. "I want our children to know both sides of their heritage." Mama C was reluctant at first, but she loved Colleen and yielded to her daughter-in-law's wishes.

The children were older now and brought their spouses to celebrate with their grandmother. Colleen's two oldest were married, and her oldest daughter, Jessica, had Colleen, a four-year-old named after her. The youngest—Paul—was still in college.

Colleen had had a hard time conceiving, and Jessica was born shortly after their seventh anniversary. Both sides of the family were anxious for offspring. "It ain't that we ain't trying," Antonio would tell both potential grandmothers with a wink. Mama C would laugh; Colleen's mother was mortified.

Their second daughter—Maureen—came two years later, and Paul two years after that. Colleen had a hysterectomy shortly thereafter—the only legitimate way she could remain in the church—as a tubal ligation was out of the question.

This Christmas was one of those watershed moments for Colleen. When she looked back years later, she realized it not only marked the end of her marriage to Antonio, but the beginning of a path she had never expected to walk.

There was another tradition at her mother's house she always looked forward to—Santa and the gift presentations. Now that her oldest daughter had a four-year-old, she could hardly wait for Santa's entrance. He usually peeked into the window first; ducking down into the bushes after one adult would point and yell, "What's that!"

Her mother's two brothers—Thomas and Patrick Campbell—were up from Florida for a visit. Tall, thin, willowy like the rest of the Campbell side of the family, they could eat a horse and never gain an ounce. Colleen had heard Uncle Thomas whisper to his brother, "That Colleen sure is a hefty one. Takes after the O'Brien's, that's fer sure."

"Idjit," Patrick whispered back. "She'll hear you."

Colleen's father usually played Santa Claus, but this year he was in the hospital after having a heart stent operation.

"Who will play Santa this year?" Thomas asked the adults who had gathered in the kitchen while Colleen's namesake slept peacefully on the sofa.

No one answered.

"I have an idea," Thomas said, grabbing Colleen by the flesh of her under arm. "Let's have Grandma Colleen do it. Why, Colleen, you wouldn't need a bit of stuffing or even a pillow like your Da has to stuff in that suit. From the looks of you, fat as you are, it would be a tight fit as it is." With that, he slapped her on the rear end and laughed.

Colleen's mother laughed too, but everyone else in the room stood silent. Colleen felt the heat of mortification crawl up her neck and onto her cheeks.

"I'll do it," Maureen's husband said. "Give me the suit and pillows."

Off he went, into the bedroom, donning the costume and going outside to look into the window of the street level apartment. His four-year-old daughter woke up about then, looked outside and said, "Why is daddy wearing a Halloween costume?"

That broke the tension in the room, but as soon as the presents were exchanged Colleen said she had a headache and asked Antonio to take her home.

In the car on the way back to New Jersey, Antonio told Colleen he was sorry for her Uncle Tommy's behavior. "He had a lot to drink. He probably won't even remember saying it in the morning."

"No, Tony. I am tired of it. I am tired of being the only fat girl in the room."

"But you are the only fat girl in the room at your mother's house. All them thin, pasty Campbell folk with their tiny bird legs—who wants that. We'll stop going, if you want. When you're with my family, we all look alike."

Colleen let the tears roll down her cheeks. Antonio noticed the drops falling on her lap. "Now, Colleen. No water works. The man is a *Ciuccio!*"

"I forgot what that means."

"Jackass," Antonio replied.

They both laughed, and drove the rest of the way home to their house in New Jersey in silence.

For the next six months, Colleen worked diligently to lose weight. She joined the program at the hospital, weighed her food, exercised, and weighed in each week. It was slow going, but by summer she had lost forty pounds.

She had wanted bariatric surgery, but knew she could never get away with it as she already had a hysterectomy, an appendectomy, and her gallbladder removed. Those were the three typical surgeries done in conjunction with "having your stomach stapled" in order to hide it from prying eyes.

She had told her best friend, Amanda. That was it. No one else would know what was going on.

Few people had noticed the change, but Antonio had insisted she go to the doctor. "You know, that is the first sign of something very wrong," he said.

"What?"

"Losing weight like this. How much have you lost? No, get on the scales and let me see."

She did, and he grabbed his head when he saw the number on the scale. "201. That's forty pounds, Colleen. You are going to the doctor. I know it's Saturday, but I have Dr. DeChaps home number. I'm calling right now."

"There is nothing wrong with me, Antonio. I am fine. I was just at the doctor in March—it's only June now. Nothing is wrong."

"I'm making you an appointment. Now."

After shouting and angry words were exchanged, Antonio headed for the telephone. As he picked up the unit to punch in the number, she grabbed his hand.

"No, don't call," Colleen said and, in a flurry of words, she finally confessed.

"What brought this on?" He was indignant now, and his words came out of curled lips in a staccato burst.

"I am tired…"

"…of being the only fat girl in the room." Antonio finished her sentence.

"Yes, and I know what you are going to say…"

"No, you don't know what I am going to say. What—now you have a boyfriend or something? My father warned me—if I didn't keep you fat, you would run off. What now, who is he?"

He had grabbed her shoulders and was shaking her. For the first time in her marriage, she was afraid.

"Stop, Antonio. Stop it!"

He suddenly realized the magnitude of his anger. He stopped and, without apology, left the house. She heard the sound of his tires squealing on the driveway. It wasn't until she was sure he was gone that she collapsed in a puddle of her own tears.

Chapter Two

Colleen had called Amanda after she was under control. Amanda agreed that it was an overreaction on Antonio's part. "He's never done this before?"

"No, nothing like this."

"Well, some men fear losing control when their wife loses weight. Remember, we talked about that last week in group."

"But Antonio? Never!"

"Well, you never know until it happens," Amanda countered. "Do you feel like driving?"

"Not really. I'm kind of shaky right now."

"I'll come and get you. It's a great day outside, and I know just the place for some tea. It's in Patterson, far enough but not too far away."

Colleen reluctantly agreed to the outing. She went into the bathroom, repaired her makeup, and put on sunglasses when she heard Amanda's car in the driveway.

*****

Amanda didn't say much on the ride to Patterson. She let her friend talk if she wanted to; otherwise the car was silent.

Finally, Colleen asked where they were going. "It's a small café with a courtyard. They serve tea, wine, and little sandwiches. Nice place for an afternoon."

The café had a small line, but it moved quickly. "We'd like a table outside," Amanda told the hostess.

"You're in luck. We have one opening up just now."

They followed the hostess to the small table for two, looked over the menu, and both ordered a crème tea. It came in a matter of minutes.

"Forget about your diet today. Nothing like scones and clotted cream to make your cares disappear."

The women at the next table were laughing and talking in high, squeaky voices about a man at another table to their right. "Look at that old fool," one said in a raspy whisper that could be heard all the way to Princeton. "Why, that young, skinny thing could be his daughter!"

"Or granddaughter," one of the others said, drawing more raucous laughter from the foursome.

Neither Amanda nor Colleen could see what was going on at the table that drew the attention from the other group. They were behind one of the large palms in a planter almost as high as the table. After listening to the group for about twenty minutes, Amanda said, "Colleen, I'm going to the ladies room. I have to see this. I'll be right back."

Colleen nodded.

But Amanda never made it to the ladies room. She came back to the table, picked up the check and frantically looked for another way out.

"What is wrong with you, Amanda?"

"Nothing. I suddenly realized I feel ill and need to get home right away. Let's get out of here."

Their waiter, seeing the commotion, walked over and asked if everything was all right. "Yes," Colleen answered. "My friend is feeling ill, and…"

It was then she turned toward the table that was the object of everyone's interest. There sat her husband Antonio with a slender girl-woman of about twenty-five. He was kissing her full on the lips, and she was stroking his hair—or what was left of it.

"I'll be right back," Colleen said.

"Colleen, don't…" Amanda words travelled on the wind because Colleen was headed full steam for the table.

"Excuse me," she said to the people at the table next to Antonio. "May I borrow this chair?"

Without waiting for an answer, Colleen swung the chair around and sat right next to Antonio and his love interest.

"Who are you," the young thing questioned.

"Hello," Colleen said as she extended her hand. "I am Antonio's wife. Colleen."

The young thing looked puzzled. She turned to Antonio. "I thought you said she was fat."

Thus ended the marriage of Colleen and Antonio Coffaro.

Colleen got the house. Antonio got the sailboat. Shortly thereafter he and Mickey (the young thing) sailed off to parts unknown.

*****

Christmas was six weeks away. Colleen had gotten over the situation with Antonio faster than she could imagine. Her work at the hospital as a ward clerk was very satisfying, and she continued with the weight loss group. She was now within twenty pounds of her goal.

Antonio called their mutual children on occasion. Colleen did not want to hear about the calls, so they stopped telling her. Mickey was still with him, apparently, and they were continuing their sailing adventure.

"Hope he drowns," Mama C said.

"No, he is your son."

"No son of mine would desert his wife."

"Well, to be fair, he offered to give her up and come back."

"I hope you told him to shove his offer."

"Well, not exactly. But it wasn't going to work. He was a control freak, and I never saw it."

They went on to discuss Christmas. "I need a change this year," Colleen said. "Amanda and her brother want me to go on a cruise with them. I think I'll do it. Tony would never go."

The cruise was over the Christmas holiday, and began in San Juan, Puerto Rico and then went to the southern Caribbean. It sounded like fun, and Amanda's brother had arranged everything. They had paid for the tickets. "I didn't know what to get you for Christmas," Amanda had said. "I think this is just what you need."

So, off they went, leaving Colleen's mother speechless and Colleen's kids to fend for themselves.

Chapter Three

Martin Standish was somewhat of a nerd. He worked in accounting at the hospital, was tall, and wore thick glasses. The glasses slipped down the oily skin on his nose and rested on the tip formed by his nostrils. It gave everyone the impression that he was frowning, which he was because the glasses weren't up on the bridge of his nose where they belonged. This, combined with a receding hairline and a complexion the color of gray modeling clay, did not make him a desirable catch.

He was forty-eight years old, never married, and lived at home with his mother. They had a two-story brownstone not far from the hospital in Clifton, New Jersey. His father, Dr. Harold Standish, had died at a medical convention in Aspen Colorado from injuries sustained in a skiing accident. His office nurse delivered the news.

Martin remembered that day well. He was twenty-two and just out of college. He summoned up the conversation his mother had on the phone with his father's nurse. "Why are you there with my husband? I thought it was a medical convention."

Nothing was ever resolved, but his mother always suspected something was going on.

His mother insisted he live at home with her until he could get on his feet. He took the job at the hospital and had been there ever since—twenty-six years this July.

Martin had dated sporadically since his father's death. His father had left half of the estate to his mother and half to a trust fund. The fund was sealed, and Martin imagined his father was providing for other offspring.

The women Martin brought home were never good enough for his mother. She would grill each woman about religion, children, her family. Nothing was a taboo subject...and none of them returned for a second round with Mrs. Standish.

"I only want what's best for you, Marty," she would say when he protested about the Standish Inquisition, as he called her line of questioning.

"I know, Mother. But why don't you give them a chance. Get to know them first. Invite them back. Be a little kinder in your approach."

Mother would smile and nod, and continue on in the same fashion. Martin finally gave up. He didn't love any of them enough to challenge his mother, risking her hysterical outbursts and a trip to the emergency room with a feigned heart attack.

Then along came Colleen O'Brien Coffaro. Red hair, blue eyes, a crazy laugh. Yes, she was a bit on the porky side, but who cared. In Martin's eyes, she was amazing.

Martin had befriended Colleen when she first came to work at the hospital fifteen years ago. They often ate lunch together (when Colleen didn't have her weight class). He was always laughing at her jokes, and she didn't pick up on the signals he was sending.

Martin was enamored from the first minute they shared lunch. After a while, he fell madly in love with Colleen. He never believed he had a chance, until one day when she told him about her husband, Antonio.

"That's terrible," he said. "Why would men do something like that?"

"Well," she had countered. "I can't speak for all men, but Antonio turned out to be a control freak. As long as I was fat, he was sure no one would look at me…not that I wanted anyone to. But apparently he had a wandering eye, and so he assumed I did, too."

She had told him about the Christmas when her uncle insisted she be Santa. "That was what did it," she said.

"Is that why you went to the program?"

"In the beginning, yes. I thought all my problems would be over if I lost weight. You know how you say, 'If only I had a size six body…' Well, it doesn't work like that."

"Where is he now?" Martin asked.

"No idea! Off sailing the seven seas with Mickey, I guess."

"So, what are you doing this holiday season?"

She told him she was having Thanksgiving with her mother, then going on a cruise with Amanda and her brother over Christmas.

"Really? Where is the cruise?"

"The Caribbean." She pulled out the brochure and showed him the route.

"Oops! Got to get back to work," Martin said after glancing at his watch.

He went back to his office, closed the door and made a reservation for the same Christmas cruise. He filled out his vacation request, went directly to his boss and got it signed, then hand carried it to Human Resources. He didn't want any chance of not getting time off.

So, off he went, making sure he wasn't on the plane with Colleen and Amanda. He wanted it to be a surprise when they ran into each other on the ship.

***

Antonio was getting bored with Mickey. She was half his age, didn't know who *The Jefferson Airplane* were, and was whiney. She didn't like the sailboat, hated the dingy and the trips to shore to get food, supplies, and do laundry. Here they were, moored at St. Thomas, and all he wanted to do was be rid of her.

It was approaching Christmas and Antonio missed Colleen, his children, and his family. They wanted nothing to do with him but had passed along the message that Colleen was taking a cruise and wouldn't be home for Christmas this year.

"Cruise? With who?"

"Amanda," his oldest daughter replied. "They're going to the Caribbean. Leaving from Puerto Rico on December nineteenth."

And just then Antonio's dim reptilian brain had a brilliant idea: He would drop Mickey at St. Thomas with enough money to get home, sail on to Basseterre, St. Kitts, and wait for the boat…and surprise his ex-wife with his presence. *What a great Christmas present for her.*

He thought Mickey would put up a stink about going back to the States, and he was stunned when she so readily said yes. He wound up giving her five thousand dollars, which was a gracious plenty, but he was glad to be rid of her and anxious to resume his life with Colleen.

He hopped a seaplane to St. Kitts, went shopping for the proper wardrobe, and purchased a ticket from a travel agent for the remainder of the cruise.

Then he waited for the arrival of the ship and his reunion with his wife.

Chapter Four

Martin did not dare tell his mother about the upcoming trip. *Knowing her, she'll want to come along.* In order to make certain she suspected nothing, he waited until she was in bed and asleep before packing. It was weeks ahead of time, but he wanted to be ready when the time came.

His plane left on December twentieth, and he had his tickets and passport hidden away in the bottom of his underwear drawer. His suitcase was under the bed, filled with his new silk pajamas and a smoking jacket. *Like Hugh Hefner—a man I greatly admire.* He didn't know why he admired him, but he sure had good luck with women. He also had a blazer and new khaki pants, together with some other items he had purchased from *The Leisure and Cruise Shoppe* in Patterson. He had Hawaiian print shirts, shorts, and sandals that the clerk helped him pick out. He was going there on a regular basis on his lunch hour to shop. He would pick up one item at a time so he could sneak them into the house under his suit jacket. He was also going to get a pedicure for the first time in his life. He wanted his toes to look a lot better if he were going to wear sandals.

The Leisure and Cruise Shoppe in Patterson was next door to the *New Jersey Pride Grocery and Delicatessen*, a place his mother regularly shopped. The bus would drop her off in front of the store. She would do her shopping and catch the bus for the return trip to their home in Patterson. Since Martin knew her schedule, and the bus schedule, he never feared running into her.

But sometimes the best laid plans run into a little snag. Such was the case one week before Martin would leave for his cruise with the unsuspecting Colleen. And so it was, on December thirteenth, Martin was coming out of *The Leisure and Cruise Shoppe* just as his mother's friend Margaret Craymore dropped Mrs. Standish off in from of the *New Jersey Pride Grocery and Delicatessen.*

To this day, both sides say they saw the other first. We do know from the accounts of witnessing bystanders that Martin attempted to melt into the brick on the outside of the building. He pressed himself against the wall, turned his head to the side, and held his breath.

It didn't work.

Mrs. Standish, seeing her son plastered against the building, began an ear-piercing squawk. "Martin. Martin. Yoo hoo! Over here. It's your mother, Martin."

"Mother," he began. "What a surprise to see you down here. Have you had your lunch?"

"Well, no. Margaret and I were just coming to town to do that very thing. We thought we'd eat here at the deli, then do our shopping. Margaret was coming anyway, and so I thought 'why not come a day early'. It seemed like a good..."

Her voice trailed off as she spied the bag in Martin's trembling hands.

She leaned over to look in the front window of *The Leisure and Travel Shoppe*. There was a mannequin dressed in a skimpy bikini. A male model was wearing a Speedo with socks stuffed in the front. A poster of a cruise ship completed the window display.

"What's in the bag, Martin?"

Martin pretended not to hear her. This was a big mistake.

"Martin! I am speaking to you," she yelled in a voice that would shatter glass. "I said, what is in that bag?" She reached for the bag, trying to pull it from his hands.

Martin only held on tighter.

"Give it to me," she squawked.

"No."

"I said, give it to me. What is in there that you cannot show your own mother."

"Nothing. But it is none of your business."

Mrs. Standish's screams and Martin's refusal had drawn a crowd. One side (mostly men) supported Martin's position, while the older women took his mother's side.

They were now in a tug-of-war over the bag. Martin had pulled his mother off her feet several times, but she refused to let go. Finally, with one last feat of super human strength, Mrs. Standish managed to wrench the bag from his hands.

Martin realized he was defeated, and slid quietly down the wall into the snow bank on the sidewalk. He covered his face with his hands and waited.

She opened the bag and pulled a pair of silk boxer shorts from the bag. On the front was an embroidered picture of Buddha with the words "rub for luck" next to it.

"What is the meaning of this," Mrs. Standish screeched, and she waved the boxer shorts to the attentive crowd.

"It's probably a joke gift for someone," a man yelled.

Martin heard him. "Yes, that's it. It's a joke gift for someone at the hospital."

"Oh. Well, I don't think that is very appropriate for a man of your breeding to give to someone."

"Mother, look…it's a joke. Now give it back."

She started to return the bag to her son when something else fell out. She ripped open one of the black sealed packets.

"What are these? Balloons?"

Martin said nothing. He knew he was doomed.

A look of panic crept across Mrs. Standish's face when she realized she was holding a condom. "Martin, these are pro-per-lack-tics."

A hush covered the crowd.

"Mother, let's talk about this at home. Please."

He managed to stand by sliding his back up the wall. He took the bag from her, returned the contents, and walked up the street to his car.

As soon as he was out of sight, Mrs. Standish wandered into *The Leisure and Travel Shoppe.*

"Hello," she said to the young man that approached her, asking if she needed assistance. "Yes, I would like to see some clothes that would be suitable for a cruise."

That evening, after a quiet dinner where neither of them spoke, Mrs. Standish decided to confront Martin.

"Martin, I understand your need for a vacation. After all, you work very hard. But why all this secrecy? You certainly don't need to hide things from me. After all, I only want what's best for you."

Years later, Martin couldn't remember if it was the brisket his mother made, the extra glass of wine, or his exhaustion after the condom incident, but he was in a sharing state of mind.

"I am going on a cruise, Mother. To the Caribbean. For seven days. To meet a woman."

"A woman? How nice. How long have you known her?"

"Seventeen years."

Seventeen years! Good God!

"I see, son. Well, that is a long time. Is she one of the young ladies you brought to the house?"

"Mother, I haven't brought anyone here to meet you for at least ten years."

"My, Martin. Has it been that long? It only seems like yesterday."

There was another uneasy silence before Mother Standish decided to continue her line of questioning.

"So, who is she?"

"I'm not going to tell you that. You'll probably call her on the phone."

"Well, it doesn't matter, dear. As long as my precious is happy. How old is she?"

"Ten years older than I am."

"Ten years! Then you won't be having children."

"No, and we won't be living here."

As soon as those words leapt from his lips, he knew he had made a big mistake.

"What do you mean? Of course you will be living here."

"Nope. She has her own house."

"I see. When do you leave?"

"It's a cruise over Christmas. I won't be here, so I'm sure Margaret will have you over. Or maybe one of your other friends."

She fought hard to retain her composure. "Well, have fun on your trip. Don't worry about me. I'll be just fine."

"Good, I know you will."

The next morning, after Martin had left for work, Mrs. Standish went through his underwear drawer. After all, since he was a child, he had always hidden things there. She found the tickets and booked a trip to the Caribbean with a flight one day before Martin's. That was so she could be on the ship, safe and sound, and see just who this woman was.

Chapter 5

December 17

The plane from Newark to Puerto Rico arrived carrying Amanda, her brother George, and Colleen. They were going to spend three days in Puerto Rico sightseeing.

December 20

Martin arrived by plane at noon. He went immediately to the ship, checked in, and stayed in his stateroom, waiting for the opportunity to run into Colleen.

Amanda, George, and Colleen checked in around four o'clock in the afternoon and went to their adjoining staterooms. They rested before dinner.

Antonio was staying in a cheap hotel in St. Kitts, his new wardrobe safely packed away in his new luggage to avoid the bed bugs residing with him in his room. That evening, he went out and purchased an engagement ring with a cubic zirconia and a wedding ring. He tried it on his little finger—that was the size Colleen had worn when they were married the first time.

December 21

The cruise shipped docked at Charlotte Amalie, St. Thomas. George had met a long lost college friend on the ship, and they were going their separate ways. This gave Colleen and Amanda plenty of time for shopping and seeing the sites.

One of the sites was Antonio's sailboat, docked at the main marina.

"What's that doing here?" Colleen said.

"What?"

"Tony's boat is moored over there."

They avoided the marina, went into town, and did some damage to their credit card accounts. They didn't see Mickey following them from a safe distance. She had decided to stay in St. Thomas and live on the boat since Antonio had paid the mooring fees for a year. Mickey did show remarkable restraint in not confronting Colleen and letting Tony's plans out of the bag.

Back on board at six o'clock that night, Colleen and Amanda were exhausted. They ate dinner in their room, as did George. Martin, dressed in his version of casual clothes, was secure behind a palm tree next to the entrance of the main dining room. He hung out for both seatings and was disturbed when Colleen was nowhere in sight.

That night, the cruise ship left St. Thomas and headed for St. Kitts Nevis where Antonio waited.

December 22

The ship docked at eight a.m. in Basseterre, St. Kitts Nevis. Antonio sat on a bench on the dock where passengers disembarked from the ship to tour the island. He watched as Colleen and Amanda, arm-in-arm, walked from the water taxi onto the island. He had grown a beard during his sailing trips, and decided not to shave until he was onboard the cruise ship. With his sunglasses, matted hair, and shorts, he looked like any homeless person.

As soon as Colleen was out of sight, he went aboard. The cruise personnel gave him a hard time because of his appearance, but he finally convinced them to let him aboard the water taxi. He made an appointment for a shave and haircut, then went to his stateroom and slept until well past seven that evening. The ship left at eight p.m. and headed for the open sea for a full twenty-four hours of travel before reaching Aruba on Christmas Eve.

December 23

There was a dance that evening in the main dining room beginning at eleven o'clock. There had been a small onboard wedding, and so the dining room was closed until 10:30 p.m. Martin waited in his room, certain that Colleen would attend the dance. She loved to dance, and he intended to make certain she had a wonderful evening.

Antonio was aroused from his sleep by a knock on the door at around nine-thirty. The attendant delivered the roses he had ordered, and the champagne in its silver bucket was placed on the table by the bed. After giving the attendant a tip, he closed the door, took the petals from two of the roses, and spread them on the bed.

Ahhh, Colleen. You are in for a treat tonight.

He popped a Viagra and proceeded to dress for the evening. His new blue blazer was a bit snug, but the others he had tried on were huge. He tied his bowtie after buttoning up the pale blue shirt. He struggled into his white linen pants, and slipped his feet into the new boat shoes he had purchased. He looked at the image in the mirror and was satisfied.

It was now 11:30. Martin and Antonio headed for the main dining room. Antonio, however, returned to his stateroom to get the ring he had purchased for Colleen. He had every intention of proposing to her in front of the other passengers. Seeing the Viagra bottle on the dresser, and forgetting he had already taken one, he popped the little pill into his mouth and followed it with a glass of water. He checked the room before leaving, making certain he had the roses wrapped in the green florist paper.

Colleen, Amanda, and George were already seated in the dining room, and the band had just finished the first number. No one was dancing (probably because it was a fast song, and most of the crowd weren't fast dancers). The younger passengers, like Colleen and Amanda, were talking and having a drink. George was scanning the room for eligible dance partners.

The second selection from the band was a slow arrangement of a Beatles song. "That's a weird arrangement," Amanda whispered.

"It is, but these folk might break a hip if they played *I Want to Hold Your Hand* at its normal tempo."

Amanda's back was to the dining room door, and Colleen had a partial view. She didn't notice the two men who arrived in the entrance at the same time. They didn't know each other, so there they stood, canvassing the room for the same woman.

"Good evening," Martin said pleasantly. "Lovely evening, isn't it?"

Antonio paused before answering. He wasn't used to men saying "lovely evening" to him. *I wonder if this guy is gay! He doesn't look gay. But then, you never can tell.*

"Yes," Antonio answered after a rather lengthy pause. "Yes, it is a lovely evening."

"Are you meeting someone?" Martin responded.

Oh, God. He is trying to pick me up! "Yes, I'm surprising someone, actually. She isn't expecting me. I'm a little nervous, so you'll excuse my lack of small talk."

"Now, isn't that interesting. I am surprising someone also. A co-worker from the hospital where we work."

"Hmmm. That's nice. I'm sure it will be a big surprise."

"Yes. I'm very excited about it."

The talk stopped as they both scanned the floor. Martin put his hand out. "By the way, I'm Martin Standish. I didn't catch your name."

That's because I didn't give it to you. Antonio pretended he didn't see Martin's outstretched hand and continued searching for Colleen.

Martin, thinking Antonio didn't hear him, touched his shoulder to get his attention. Antonio jumped back. "Hey, buddy."

"I said, I'm Martin Standish. I didn't catch your name." He waved his hand in front of Antonio's startled face, forcing him to look at his outstretched hand.

"Tony. Hey, ah, Martin. I gotta go. Nice talking with you."

Antonio walked around the side of the room to get a better view of the room. The place was packed and was a sea of white hair. *Colleen's red hair should stand out nicely.*

Meanwhile, Martin had gone in the other direction searching for Colleen. He was to the right of the stage, leaning against the wall and moving his head back and forth in an attempt to scan the entire area.

The band stopped and announced they were taking a break. As soon as the crowd was seated, Martin saw her. She was sitting with her friend from the hospital, Amanda, and another man. They were laughing and talking in that way old friends do who know each other well.

For a brief moment Martin panicked. What if the man was with Colleen? What if they were on this trip together? *Oh, God! What have I done!*

A woman had walked over to the table, and the man with Colleen and Amanda stood up and kissed her. They walked off together.

With that, Martin started toward the table.

After he was half way across the dance floor, he noticed Tony who had been standing at the door with the red roses. He was headed in the same direction. Tony looked up to see Martin, and he began walking faster. Martin, assuming Tony was headed for Colleen, broke into a trot.

They were within fifty paces of Colleen's table, when a woman darted out of nowhere and grabbed Martin by the back of his coat. Martin, intent on getting to Colleen before Tony, didn't notice anyone was hanging on his coat tails until he heard a familiar voice squealing his name. He stopped so quickly that his mother flew through his legs and landed under Colleen's chair.

The sliding into the table didn't faze Mrs. Standish. She reached up and pinched Amanda on the thigh. Amanda looked at the woman staring up at her from under the table. "What's the matter with you!" she said.

"You hussy! Trying to take Martin away and move him into your house. You're a Jezebel."

"Whoa. What are you talking about?"

By this time both Martin and Antonio had arrived at the table. Martin said, "Not her, Mother. Her!" and he pointed to Colleen.

Tony, assuming that Martin was after him, fell into the chair vacated by George. "Colleen, I love you. This man has been trying to pick me up."

"I what!" Martin said.

"You asked me if I was meeting someone here, and you put your arms on me."

"I did not! I assumed you were meeting someone because of the flowers."

Mrs. Standish was crawling toward Colleen, her pincher fingers ready. "Mother, stop it. I see what you're doing."

Caught in the act, Mrs. Standish lay prone on the floor.

"Tony, what are you doing here?" Colleen asked.

"I am here to win you back. I have our room all prepared. Rose petals on the bed. Here…" He extended to roses to his ex-wife. "And I have something else." He reached into his pocket and pulled out the engagement ring.

Dropping to one knee, he said, "Will you please marry me?"

"She's already married," Amanda said.

"What?" all three of the interlopers said in unison.

The band was back on the stage, and the singer walked to the microphone. "Ladies and gentlemen, we had a lovely wedding before the dance this evening. Our couple is here tonight, and they are going to have their first dance as a married couple. Please welcome to the floor Colleen O'Brien Coffaro and her partner for life, Amanda Louise Harris."

And Colleen and Amanda danced the night away.

This story is dedicated to my LGBT friends who this year won the right to marry the person they love regardless of their gender.

GROWING TOGETHER,
GROWING APART

JULIE LEVERENZ

Chapter One

Jacky Nic steered his second-hand pickup onto Canon Boulevard. On the seat beside him, the morning's *Daily Press* lay open to the Help Wanted classifieds. It was noon on a crisp fall day, and two women were striding down the sidewalk, their sun hats bobbing in sync with the arms swinging at their sides. Recognizing them as he drove past, he tapped his horn and stuck his arm out the window in upraised greeting.

But his face was grim as he watched his coworkers' colorful hats receding in his rear view mirror. Was it so wrong of him to want his beloved Missy to have what those women had? Instead of being cooped up in a rented house in Denbigh, Missy could be out there with an interesting job, like them. What had happened to her hopes, the ones she'd whispered to him on those lazy summer afternoons along the Pearl River? Now that he, little Jacques Nicolas from the Bayou, was at last living his dream, he wanted Missy to realize hers, too.

Stopping for a red light on Victory Boulevard, he remembered exactly when his plans had first been sidelined: that dreadful day in tenth grade when his Papa died. To support his *maman* and sisters, he'd had to quit school and work the waterfront. Then Hurricane Katrina had chased them here to Newport News, Virginia, where his uncle was stationed at Fort Eustis. Last year, his sisters and maman moved back to Louisiana, and Maman begged him to go home, too, but there weren't any steady jobs on the Bayou. None that paid like this one, anyway. Besides, he owed Symbics; after hiring him as a stockroom clerk, the company had pushed him to get his GED, paid for his Associates Degree at Thomas Nelson Community College, and promoted him. Twice.

At least that's what he had told Maman and his sisters. The real reason he wouldn't go back was that Missy Lafont wasn't there.

Jacky glanced at the tattoo that decorated the chestnut-colored skin on his forearm: "Missy" in curly script. Ah, Missy, his high school sweetheart—the prettiest, sweetest, most perfect girl any guy could dream of. Katrina had torn her from him; he'd heard her family had fled to Texas, but he'd never been able to find out where. None of the online databases that he checked regularly had found Missy or her family in Texas, Louisiana, Wisconsin, anywhere. He couldn't imagine walking the roads back home, seeing her shadow around every corner. The cavernous hole in his heart never got smaller.

Then, last December, he yielded to Maman's insistence that he come home for Christmas. It was just as painful as he'd feared: the Parish was a shell of its former self, with only rubble left of the homes where he and his *copains* had laughed and played. Missy's house was gone, and Maman lived in one of the new, sterile, packing-box houses that dotted the streets. It didn't feel like home, not anymore.

But the church had survived, and Father Martin Boudreaux was still admonishing his flock with sharp, witty sermons. On Christmas Eve, the music and rituals of the familiar service brought back memories of Jacky's boyhood, sitting in the sanctuary with his parents and sisters. When Father Martin caught his eye and winked, Jacky thought, *Maybe there is a little bit of home left here, after all.*

After the service, Jacky allowed his mother to push him through the milling throng and show him off to her friends.

"Oh! Jacques, *quel grand homme*," the women exclaimed, touching his cheek and tousling his hair as if he were still four years old, even though they had to reach up to do so. He smiled, complimented the ladies, and asked about their children, his old buddies. But whenever he started to ask about Missy Lafont, Maman would propel him on to meet someone else.

Suddenly, from behind him, a hand touched his tattoo, sending an electric current down his arm. Jacky whirled around, and there was Missy. He must have looked stupid or something, because her smile faltered when she said, "Hey, Jacky Nic."

"Hey, Missy." It was all he could manage; his tongue didn't work. He'd been praying for this moment for years. Years! And here she was, an apparition, even more beautiful than he remembered.

"Surprise," Maman said, giving Jacky's arm a playful punch and engulfing Missy in a bear hug. Missy beamed at Jacky over Maman's shoulder. She raised her left hand. It was ring-less. Jacky grinned and raised his. Missy's eyes filled and Jacky wrapped his arms around both of them, his dear

Maman and his beloved Missy. *Thank you, Lord Jesus. Thank you.*

They were married three months later in a joyful, music-filled ceremony; even Father Martin danced at the reception. After a quick trip to Disney World, Jacky and Missy settled into their little house in Denbigh. Every day, Jacky and Missy praised God's goodness.

***

But between Katrina and now, something had derailed Missy's whispered dreams, and today, Jacky had resolved that he was going to find out what it was. Having jobs was what women did these days, yet every time he brought it up in the few months they'd been married, Missy shrugged him off or changed the subject. Pulling into the driveway of their one-bedroom bungalow, he tucked the newspaper under his arm, collected the lunch box that Missy had so lovingly prepared for him that morning, and let himself in the front door, calling, "*Allô*, Missy—I come to have lunch with my bride."

"Jacky? *C'est toi? Quelle surprise!*" Missy emerged from the bedroom, flustered, still wearing the filmy gown she had slept in the night before. She brushed a lock of dark hair from her forehead. "I was just taking a little rest, is all." She spotted his lunch box. "Ah, go, you, and eat. Give me *un moment*, I will dress and join you."

Instead, Jacky guided Missy into the living room and made her sit on the dainty brocade armchair that she had fallen in love with at Haynes Furniture. Seating himself on the footstool before her, he took her hand, concerned.

"You are feeling well?"

Missy laughed. "Oh yes. All good. I was just reading a little and next thing I'm asleep." She moved to get up. "I go dress now."

Jacky put his hand out and stopped her. "I want to talk to you." He held up the newspaper, showing the four ads that he had circled. He inclined his head to the table in the dining ell, where another copy of the paper lay untouched from where he had left it that morning.

Missy paled. "I hadn't gotten to it yet." Then she brightened. "You found some good ones?" She reached for the paper, but Jacky set it down on the floor.

"There have been many good ones," he said. "What's going on, Chérie? Your wonderful degree in medical technology; your dream of working in a big hospital—you say you want to find a job, but there are always excuses."

Missy hung her head. "You are angry with me."

"Oh no, not angry, Missy." Jacky took both of her hands in his. "Never angry. Just *curieux*. There is something you aren't telling me?"

Missy raised her head, but her eyes drifted past him. He saw her weighing her answer. When her eyes met his, he saw hesitation and then resolve.

"*Non*, there is nothing to tell," she said. "Your Missy is just a silly, lazy, *petite fille*." She glanced down at her nightgown, as if it explained everything. "Go," she said firmly. "Eat your lunch. One minute to dress and we will look at these *fantastique* jobs you have found."

Chapter Two

Back on Canon Boulevard, the two women that Jacky had passed were halfway through their lunchtime walk. Louisa Danby loped along in a red canvas Scala hat that contrasted garishly with her DayGlo orange down vest. Beside her, Katherine Stokely lengthened her steps to keep up, wearing a deep teal floppy hat that coordinated perfectly with her windbreaker.

"You seem preoccupied today," Louisa said. "I've been yammering on about my crazy family coming for Thanksgiving and you haven't said more than two words since you told me who that guy was in the red pickup truck."

A biochemist, Louisa had worked at Symbics for four years. She hadn't really connected with any of her coworkers, though, until Katherine had come around to her lab last summer and asked how attached Louisa was to her little desktop printer. "Very attached," Louisa had said emphatically. And yet somehow Katherine had persuaded her, and everybody else at Symbics, that getting off their duffs and stepping out to use a regional printer would make them healthier, happier, and richer. Well, maybe not rich— Katherine said Symbics was the one saving a boatload of money on the deal. Last month, Katherine had suggested trading their lunchtime lattes for healthy hikes, and so here they were.

Surprised that Louisa had read her bleak mood so easily, Katherine forced a laugh and changed the subject. "I can't believe you don't know Jacky Nic. Lord, before he got married every unattached woman at Symbics was after him. Probably some of the married ones, too." Katherine babbled on, to prove she wasn't at all preoccupied. "His wife's too adorable for words, a brunette Barbie doll, but shy and sweet, if you can imagine. She brought the most amazing chocolate cupcakes to the picnic last month." Katherine gave Louisa a cheery grin.

Louisa slanted her eyes at her friend. "Nice try," she said. "So what is going on with you?"

A car turned in front of them and Katherine put her arm out to prevent Louisa from stepping into its path. After they crossed Bluecrab Road safely, Louisa cleared her throat. "Ahem?" she said.

Seeing that Louisa wouldn't let it go, Katherine took a moment to decide where to start. Finally she said, "Was it horrible when you got your Ph.D.? I mean, were you working crazy hours and miserable all the time?"

"Miserable? I'm not sure that's the word. It was crazy, sure, and my dissertation advisor drove me four ways from insane, but I had some great times, too." Louisa looked over at Katherine. "Why do you ask?"

"Oh, Anders got on my case last night about how much harder he has it than I do." Katherine's husband was a marine biologist working on his doctorate at the Chesapeake Marine Institute. He and Katherine had met at Duke University and married six years ago, right after graduation. For the first five years of their marriage, while Anders pursued his studies,

Katherine worked at the College of William and Mary and went to night school for her MBA. Last January, she had landed the job at Symbics, where she was an Operations Coordinator.

"I thought he finished his dissertation?" Louisa said. "I was over the moon when I finally turned mine in."

"He did, but we got into a pissing contest last night about whose work is more important."

"Uh oh," said Louisa. "What happened?"

"Well, yesterday I worked late. He got peeved. Does Max mind when you work late?" Max, Louisa's husband, was an orthodontist.

Louisa considered the question. "Sure," she said. "Especially when I forget to call. But he stays late with patients, too. I guess when you marry a professional, it's part of the package."

While she thought about this, Katherine tilted the brim of her hat to block the sun better. "Problem is," she said, "I wasn't a professional when Anders married me. But work has grown on me. Makes me feel like I'm worth something, you know?"

"Yeah, I hear you," said Louisa. "But you two were fine at your party, right?" Katherine nodded. She and Anders had thrown a Halloween Party, and Max and Anders had hit it off. Louisa said, "Maybe he's just decompressing. Post-dissertation depression or something."

Katherine was unconvinced. "Maybe."

Louisa teased, "Max and I have a spare room if you ever need it." She gave Katherine's arm a reassuring pat. "Hey, hang in there. Anders is a great guy. You can work it out."

Louisa's pat landed on the red, swollen bruise on Katherine's arm. Somehow, she managed not to flinch.

***

That afternoon, Katherine had trouble concentrating on her work. She kept replaying the night before and wishing she could have shared the details with Louisa. But no. *Louisa thinks Anders is a great guy.* Katherine had to figure this out on her own.

It had started when she opened the front door and Anders yelled down the hall, "Where've you been, Kat? A guy could starve to death around here."

"Sorry," she yelled back. "I had to finish up a project."

Anders came out of the back room. His lanky, six foot four inch frame filled the hallway, and he glared at her with the inborn assurance of someone whose family traced back to the Mayflower and summered in the Hamptons. Whenever he did that, she was painfully reminded of growing up with one pair of shoes and a threadbare coat two sizes too big—a girl whose Dad worked in a coal mine and died of black lung; whose brother died of a drug overdose; whose full ride at Duke had been scarred by her poverty and unfamiliarity with How Things Are Done. Where would she be if he hadn't taken her under his wing then fallen in love with her?

"You couldn't call?" His tone implied unspeakable rudeness.

"I did call. You didn't pick up. I sent a text, too." Katherine's voice trembled.

Anders pulled out his phone, switched it on, and shook his head in disgust. "You know I turn my phone off when I'm working."

"Right, sorry," she said, and turned to the kitchen, hoping to forestall a lecture. "Dinner in fifteen."

"Hold up," Anders said. "It's past time for you to get your priorities straight. Family first, then work, right?"

Katherine stopped. *Here it comes.* "Of course," she said. "But—"

"But?" he challenged. "How can there possibly be a 'but'? Your work is a diversion, remember—something to do until I get my degree and we settle down somewhere and have a family." He stared down at her. "That was what you wanted, right? Or have you forgotten that was always the plan?"

"Oh, I remember," Katherine said, her face growing hot. "And I remember you egging me on to get that MBA because I would make a lot more money. And now it seems like the money is all you care about."

Anders narrowed his eyes. "What do you mean by that?"

"I mean that you've never taken any interest in my work." Katherine took a deep breath to build up her courage. "Guess what—I discovered that I like working. You've been so wrapped around your own that you haven't noticed, have you?"

"Oh, I've noticed," Anders barked. "I see you coming home late, slapping any old thing on the table for supper so you can get back to the so-called work you drag home in that briefcase. I see you rushing off in the morning like you can't wait to get there."

Katherine couldn't believe what she was hearing. "What about your late nights with your dissertation advisor, and rushing off to Beaufort and Woods Hole like you can't wait to get there? Am I not allowed to like my work as much as you like yours?"

Anders grabbed Katherine's arm and squeezed, hard. "Who says I like my work?" he roared. "The last six years have been a brutal slog, not a walk in the park. It's what scientists do: we put up with a lot of crap so we can maybe, someday, make a tiny difference in how people understand the world."

Katherine was frightened, and her arm hurt where Anders was gripping it. She held up her other hand. "Quit, Andy, you're hurting me."

Anders flung away her arm in disgust. "You can't possibly understand," he said. "Not when you're all whoop-de-do about printers, for Christ's sake. Things will change around here: you're my wife, we have a plan, and I expect you to follow it. Now go make supper, I'm hungry." He reached for the TV remote.

***

Now, almost a day later, Katherine's mind still churned with scathing retorts: *You're my husband—how dare you talk to me like that. There are tons of scientists at Symbics; they're doing important stuff that might change the world, and printers help them do it.*

But a truth niggled at the back of her mind. As a girl, growing up in western Pennsylvania, her dream had always

49

been to marry someone brilliant and have a smart, rowdy passel of kids. If she worked, she would have a fall-back kind of job, one that would give her flexibility when they had a family.

Katherine considered the possibility that maybe Anders had reason to be upset. Liking her work turned the plan on its end, didn't it, and Anders hadn't had a say. Above all, Katherine wanted them to be fun and loving Kat'n'Andy again, the inseparable couple that had been the envy of all their friends in college. She was his wife and his partner, and she loved him; surely they could work this out together.

She looked at the papers strewn about her desk, wondering how she could do all this and be the wife that Anders wanted, too. Well, Louisa did it; every working woman had to figure that out, didn't she? *Time management. Project management. Smarter not harder. Multitasking*—the old MBA clichés rumbled through her head. She rubbed her forehead, where an ache was beginning to grow. *Uh oh.* She had been getting these headaches more and more often. After downing a couple of Excedrin, she pulled out a piece of paper and started to make a list.

That night, Katherine set the table with extra care, using the blue and white wedding china and a real tablecloth instead of the usual vinyl or place mats. She was stirring the spaghetti sauce when Anders crept up behind her and put his hands lightly over her eyes. "Guess who?" he said.

Katherine jumped, then giggled. "Matt Damon?"

"Thanks for not saying Darth Vader," Anders said, bending down to kiss her neck. "Although I can totally see you as Princess Leia." He stroked her long brown hair.

Katherine felt some of the tension drain away that she had carried for the past twenty-four hours. Here was Anders being his charming, goofy self again. She laughed and said, "Yeah, right. Me, a fearless Jedi warrior? I don't think so." She picked up a long spoon to stir the boiling spaghetti and watched the long strands of pasta swirl hypnotically while Anders' fingers played with her hair. "Mm, don't stop," she said.

He started massaging the tops of her shoulders. Katherine leaned back against his chest and closed her eyes for a moment. When his hand grazed the bruise on her arm she twitched, and he quickly moved it away.

"You okay?" he whispered.

Six years of marriage had taught Katherine much about her husband, and she understood that this was his way of apologizing.

If you can apologize, I can forgive, she thought as she dumped the half-cooked spaghetti in the strainer, shut off the stove, and gave her husband a passionate kiss.

Later, over reheated spaghetti, Katherine marveled at the way Anders knew exactly how to push her buttons, for better or for worse. Tonight was definitely for better. She reached her hand across the table. "I love you, Anders Stokely," she said.

With a tender smile, Anders took her hand. "I love you, too, Kat." But Katherine detected something in his light blue eyes—something held back, as if she were being put on probation.

Chapter Three

On a frosty Saturday morning two weeks before Christmas, Missy hugged herself on the front stoop while Jacky backed his truck out of the driveway. A fat Styrofoam snowman sat on the concrete at her feet; behind her, an apple-studded wreath decorated the front door. Jacky blew Missy a kiss and laughed at her two-handed, over-the-top reply kisses. Ah, Missy, how he adored her—he might as well be off to slay dragons instead of going to get an oil change.

But Jacky was baffled, wondering what else he could do. As far as he could tell, Missy hadn't made even one call responding to a help-wanted ad. At least she took care to get dressed first thing every morning, but for the life of him he had no idea how she spent her days. Missy cooked—*mon dieu,* how she could cook—but she paid little attention to the house. Dust, clutter, and dirty clothes didn't seem to bother her. One day, he realized that she had worn the same dress for three days in a row. Remembering his mother's admonition to him and his sisters when they complained that they had no clean clothes for school, or the car needed gas— "If something bothers you it is yours to fix,"—Jacky found himself doing the dusting and the laundry as well.

Yet Missy was loving, cheerful, and wonderful to talk to. She was interested in his work and made thoughtful—even helpful—comments and questions. He told himself he should be thrilled to have such a beautiful devoted wife. And yet, somewhere in the back of his mind lurked a feeling of dismay at being so much the center of her universe. More and more, he felt it as a burden.

When he returned, Jacky stepped into the kitchen to find Missy on the phone, saying sharply, "Non, *absolument pas*, Maman. You must not tell him."

Jacky hesitated fractionally, then said in a hearty voice, "Tell me what?" Missy whirled around. He laughed, choosing not to see the shock on her face. "Okay, what mischief are you and your maman plotting?"

"Jacky, he is home," Missy said into the phone. Her voice sounded strangled. She disconnected and put on a cheery face. "You are soon back," she said to Jacky.

"Tell me what?" Jacky repeated.

"Oh, *rien*, we are just deciding our special treats when we go home for Noel," Missy said.

Jacky heard a hollowness in her tone. He hung the truck keys on the hook by the door then sat down at the kitchen table. Willing himself not to assume anything, he folded his hands in his lap and said quietly, "Tell me what, Missy?"

Missy drew a shaky breath. She started to shrug, as she had so many times before. Jacky would have none of it—he shook his head to caution her: no more lies.

Missy understood; he saw her face crumple with indecision. Instinctively, Jacky pushed his chair back from the table, drew Missy into his lap, and cradled her like a small child. She tucked her face into the crook of his neck and, after a long moment, began to speak.

"There was *un garçon*," Missy started, her voice small and hesitant. "In Texas. Two years ago." She must have felt Jacky stiffen, because she said quickly, "I did not know where you were, or if I would ever see you again."

Jacky forced himself to acknowledge that Missy was right; he had had no claim on her then. He stroked her thick, wavy hair. "Please go on, Chérie."

"I met him at school. He was *gentil*, treated me nice. Other men, not so nice, try to follow me, make me like them." She shuddered. "He shoo them off, walk me home after night class. After some months, we got engaged. Maman did not like him, but I thought she was just unhappy that I would leave her." Jacky felt Missy grow tense in his arms. She plucked at a stray thread on her sleeve.

Jacky waited. He did not like the sound of this, not at all.

Missy felt as tight as a coiled spring when she blurted, "Before we were married I... I became *enceinte*. Pregnant."

Stunned, Jacky struggled between wanting to push her away and hold her close. An incoherent cry escaped him. In desperation, he fixed his gaze on the vinyl flooring and its fake tiles in blue, gold, and tan. The design had worn through in front of the sink. His tongue felt wooden, but he had to know. "Go on," he croaked.

Missy continued, talking into Jacky's collarbone. "When I told him about the *bébé*, he said I must stop school right away to take care of him and the child. But I did not want to do that. I told him I could have a job and still be a good maman to our bébé, and a good wife to him. He became very angry. Maman warned me, but I thought he would change." She made a little cry, like a lost kitten. "I thought that my love could make him understand. I thought that he loved me."

Jacky studied the scuffed spot in front of the sink.

"I tried, I really did," she said. "But he would not listen. The bigger my *grossesse*, the angrier he got. He became a crazy man; his eyes—he looked at me like I was *un objet*, not *une femme*. I never thought—" Missy stuttered, "how could... but he did. He hit me. I lost my bébé." She began to sob.

Jacky felt Missy's grief vibrate through his body as if he were observing from a distance.

"And that's when you came back to the Parish," he said, his voice flat. "To escape from him." Missy bowed her head. An unaccustomed anger gripped him. He lifted Missy's chin, looked in her eyes, and said, "What happened to this man?" As he said it, he knew he was asking the wrong question.

Missy said, "My brothers—they did something. They would not say. He did not bother me again."

"*Tes frères*—your brothers knew," Jacky stated. Missy nodded, not meeting his eyes. "*Ta* maman knew." She nodded again. "And you could not tell me?" He could not keep the hurt and, yes, anger, out of his voice.

Missy quailed. "I thought, how can you still love me if you know this terrible thing?" Tears coursed down her cheeks. Without thinking, Jacky reached over to the countertop and handed her a tissue.

"Your maman wanted to tell me?" he said.

Missy held the tissue, not bothering to dab at her streaming eyes. She dipped her head. "It is such a burden, this secret. She said you would understand. It is why I cannot look for a job. I see men's eyes on me, like hunter's eyes, and they are the eyes he had. I used to want to work, and I know you want me to, but I feel like a dove, waiting for the gunshot." She looked up, pleading through her tears, "I did right to tell you, Jacky?"

Emotions flooded him, each one claiming primacy: anger, sympathy, betrayal, fear. Lifting her gently from his lap, he set her on her feet. Considering the young, beautiful woman who stood trembling before him, Jacky wondered if he really knew his wife at all. He shook his head as if to clear it. "I am a man. I cannot... I don't know, Missy. I just don't know." Jacky raised his hand halfway, then turned and left the room.

***

At the other end of the house, Jacky buried his head in a pillow to block out the sound of Missy's wracking sobs. He couldn't think, he couldn't speak; he was numb as Missy's secret bore into him and walled off a big chunk of his heart.

That night, Jacky feigned sleep when Missy came to bed, then he lay awake, listening to her as she cried a little, then finally drifted off. The sheet moved when her foot twitched, and she gave a long, dreamy sigh. He could not shake thoughts of her just like this—making slow, soft, sweet breaths, in and out—in another bed, beside another man. He could not stop thinking of that man's hands on her.

That night, and every night after, Jacky's thoughts tormented him. It was his fault: he had not protected her. He should have married her before Katrina. He should have followed her to Texas. He should have found her sooner. *Should, should, should.* And then, inevitably, his mind circled back to Missy. *And yet, when I did find her, she wouldn't tell me. She doesn't trust me. She's afraid of me. She doesn't believe in me.*

During the day, Jacky and Missy went through the motions—polite conversation, compliments on the food. No eye contact, no touching, not even an inadvertent brush of the fingers when a plate was passed. Understanding that their future was in his hands, Jacky felt like he was suspended by a slender thread poised to snap and bring him crashing down to destroy them both.

Chapter Four

Two days later, Katherine barged into her boss's office and shooed the secretary out with a, "'Scuse us, would you? I'm having a meltdown here." Slamming the door, she howled, "How could he do that?"

"He who? Do what?" her boss said. Allen Ostrow was almost as round as he was tall, with a combover that made him look ten years older than his forty-five years. He fancied vests and bow ties, earning him the nickname "Tweedledum." A helicopter beanie hung jauntily on the coat rack by his door. But today Katherine didn't want Tweedledum; she needed The Terminator.

"Your boss, Blankenship," Katherine said, pacing. "I quote: 'That was a nice presentation, Katherine, but we need that money for something else.'"

Allen put his hands out, palms up. "God, I'm sorry. Blankenship is the president's hatchet man, and the Pres must not have wanted it for some reason."

Katherine slumped into a chair, shaking her head. "He let me go through the whole thing. The whole thing, for God's sake, right in front of the president and all the vice presidents, and then he yanked the rug out."

Last summer, Katherine had been amazed that Allen let her do the presentation on regional printers to the Management Council by herself, but he'd said that was how it worked at Symbics. "You do the work, you make the presentation, you get the credit." That time, the Council had barely let her finish before they approved the proposal.

Now, Katherine was fuming. "Didn't he hand us the day care project, right here in this office? Didn't he go through it with me, just last week?" *Onsite day care—you make the presentation, you take the fall.* "I feel like such an idiot."

"You gave it your best shot, Kat," Allen said. "And nobody will think any less of you. You're in good company— I've been there; I doubt there's a manager here who hasn't been blindsided at some point." He glanced at his watch. "It's just after four. Didn't you tell me the Chesapeake Marine Institute is having their holiday party tonight?"

Katherine nodded, glum.

"Go," said Allen. "It's Friday. Party with your husband. Forget Symbics even exists for a couple of days."

***

An hour later, after sitting for what seemed like forever on the Coleman Bridge while it opened for a Navy ship headed for the Weapons Station up the York River, Katherine dragged herself into the house. "Andy?" She looked in the lean-to by the back door; his bicycle wasn't there. Unwilling to face the empty house, she drove to the Marine Institute, thinking she could help set up for the party, or at least visit with Anders.

Since their blowup over her working late, and their makeup during the postponed spaghetti supper, Katherine had paid close attention to his moods. Most of the time, he was loving, kind, and funny—even silly; they spent many evenings convulsed in laughter. Most of the time, she was able to caress or banter away the occasional scowls that tightened his face, as she had since their dating days. But some of the time, his scowls now flared into anger, even rage. At night, while she lay in bed and listened to his regular breathing, she worried about the times when she hadn't read him right, when she should have said something different— funnier, wiser, dumber?—to short-circuit his fury. Above all, she was learning never to raise her voice, never to contradict. Two days ago he had pushed her off the chair and skinned her knee.

Still, there were plenty of good days. With luck, this would be one of them. *He'll probably be thrilled to hear about the lousy meeting,* she thought. *Too many more days like this one and I'll happily become a backup-job wife.* Maybe she could even cadge a hug.

She parked in the Institute lot. Unlike Anders, who had never seen Katherine's workplace, Katherine often visited the Institute and knew most of his coworkers. She found three of them—all women, she noted wryly—spreading red and green plastic covers on tables in the lobby. Katherine chatted with them, then went to find Anders.

The door to the grad students' office was closed. Katherine gave a quick knock, opened it, and froze. On one of the desks, a buxom woman with a mass of blonde curls gave a yelp and pushed Anders off her. Anders looked at the blonde, confused, and then saw Katherine. His face darkened.

Katherine rushed out the door and down the hall. Hurrying through the lobby, she never saw the sad, sympathetic faces of the three women who paused to watch her. She jumped in the car and drove blindly, not caring where she went.

She drove north, taking Business Highway 17 when it veered into Gloucester Courthouse. On Main Street, the neon sign of a new shop caught Katherine's eye: the Silver Boutique. On impulse, she pulled into the parking lot. She needed something to keep her brain from imploding.

Inside the shop, she glanced over the glass-encased jewelry cabinets then gravitated to the displays of scarves, purses, and other accessories. A sleek blue Lily Pulitzer scarf with whorls of bright green and pink caught her eye. She looked at the price tag: $108. Katherine blinked. *Anders would kill me.* Then she remembered.

She took the scarf over to the counter. "I'll take this one, please."

For supper, she sat at the bar in Applebee's and ordered wine, an appetizer, entrée, and dessert. The bar was busy, and she struck up amiable conversations with a series of couples on either side of her. Once in a while she checked her cell phone, but it was silent: no texts, no calls. When she left the bar at ten-thirty, she eyed the Hampton Inn across the street, debating whether she should get a room for the night. *Or the rest of my life,* she thought. But no, she had as much right to stay in the house as Anders. She would go home and hear what he had to say.

Finding the house dark and empty, Katherine was more relieved than worried. She carefully folded her new scarf in her lingerie drawer then settled down with a paperback for an hour before going to bed.

When she woke on Saturday morning, Anders snored beside her, reeking of alcohol. Disgusted, Katherine got up and dressed. From habit, after eating a breakfast of granola and banana, she straightened the living room, then closed the bedroom door and ran the vacuum. Anders did not emerge. She took the shopping list and went to Food Lion.

The headache hit her in the bread aisle. Drilling straight through her temples, it felt like it was sucking her eyes deep into their sockets. Abandoning her cart, Katherine hurried to the car, grabbed the bottle of water in the console, swallowed two Excedrin, and pressed her forehead against the steering wheel. *Go away go away go away*, she chanted, tracking the minutes on her watch.

Half an hour later, when she lifted her head, her stomach lurched and bile rose in her throat. She felt dizzy. Frightened, she looked around, wondering if she should call Anders, or 911. Her eyes lighted on a square brick building across the parking lot: "Urgent Care."

Two hours later, when she returned home with the groceries and a bottle of prescription pills, Anders and his bicycle were gone.

***

That evening, the sky was dark when the back door banged and Anders came into the kitchen. Katherine was standing at the cupboard, deciding whether to eat in or go back to Applebee's. She turned to face him, keeping her expression blank.

He said, "They were asking where you were, at the party."

Katherine said nothing. *He doesn't even have the grace to look abashed*, she thought.

"Where were you?" he demanded.

"Out," she said, then countered, "I assume the party didn't last until all hours. Where were you?"

"Out," he mimicked.

Katherine was silent. After a moment, Anders tilted his head and said, "I gather that you are upset." He took a step toward her and reached out his hand. "Well, don't be. She was nothing. It's no big deal."

Katherine stepped away. "That's it?" she said. "Does 'she' know she's nothing? It looked like more than nothing to me."

Anders laughed. "Hey," he said, spreading his arms wide, "the girl wouldn't leave me alone. What's a red-blooded guy supposed to do? It was just a kiss, for God's sake." His face grew serious. "You're my wife, Kat, nothing's going to mess with that." He clasped his hands in front of his chest in supplication. "Forgive?"

Katherine studied him. *It's not that easy*, she thought. For a few long moments, she let him stew. Finally she said, "I ate at Applebee's last night. I'm thinking about going back there tonight. You can come if you want."

With a hint of apprehension, Anders said, "Sounds like a plan."

"And I want to tell you about my horrible day at work yesterday, and you have to listen and be sympathetic."

"Deal. Anything else?"

It didn't escape her that Anders' concern was only for himself. But he looked so dadgum pitiful standing there, with his eyes all droopy and pleading. *That blonde probably did throw herself at him*, she thought. Plus, it felt good to be in the driver's seat for a change.

"Not a word about how much I spent on the scarf I bought," she said.

Chapter Five

By Monday morning, Katherine and Anders had struck a kind of truce. Yesterday they had brought home a fir tree, wrestled it into the living room, and decorated it to the sounds of festive carols. By the end of the day, the peace and joy of the season had crept into the most skeptical corner of her heart. She wanted to believe that the blonde had indeed been "nothing," so she allowed herself to give him the benefit of the doubt.

As for the headache, well, she never got around to telling him about it. The doc-in-a-box had given her a miraculous drug that made it disappear—poof—and now she had some pills for the next time. She was afraid Anders would use the headaches against her: yet another argument for getting her back in line.

But the closer she drove on her commute to Symbics, the more apprehensive she became. She was sure that everyone would know about her humiliation before the Management Council, and that they would treat her with excessive kindness or whisper behind her back. In the parking lot, she sat in her car for a moment, gave herself a little pep talk, and plastered a smile on her face before getting out and heading for the entrance.

When she got to her cubicle, Katherine had a voice mail from Louisa, "Hey, Kat, I heard about the debacle. Call me; I can't wait till lunch to know what you bought." But before she had a chance to call back, Allen appeared in her doorway.

"So, what did you buy?" he said.

Katherine was baffled. "What makes you think I bought anything?"

Allen guffawed. "Because I got a Seiko watch. Ellena from Personnel bought herself a fur coat. I think it was diamond earrings or something for Michelle in Safety. Ralph in Engineering got a Shimano fishing rod. Everybody buys something when they get creamed by the Management Council."

Katherine shook her head in amazement. Instead of going down as a black mark on her record, her disgrace had initiated her into some kind of elite society. "A hundred-dollar scarf and the works at Applebee's," she said. "Twice."

Allen gave her a high five. "Welcome to the club," he said.

Katherine didn't tell him that she'd had two reasons to indulge herself this weekend. Maybe she should have bought two scarves.

Allen changed the subject. "You're coming to the party Friday, right?"

The Operations Division Christmas party was traditionally held in a local nightspot, but in the mid-afternoon. Dates and spouses were discouraged from coming, and Katherine had heard that the parties were fabulous, both of which puzzled her. Work parties were by definition anything but "fabulous," and how many significant others would happily stay home while their partners-spouses partied without them?

"Sure, wouldn't miss it," she said, figuring the odds that Anders would want to come were slim to none.

***

Two days later, on Wednesday evening, Anders burst from the front door as soon as Katherine turned into the driveway. He pulled her out of the car and wrapped her in a big, bouncing hug. "Great news," he whooped, "Woods Hole wants me to start in January."

"What?" Katherine said, trying to wrap her head around his words. "That's amazing, Andy. What's the job?" Walking to the house, Anders filled her in, and Katherine grappled with the implications. A possible snag leapt to her mind. "But what about your dissertation defense?" His defense was scheduled in February.

"Oh," he said dismissively, "I'll be on probation, and passing that will be part of the deal. Besides, nobody ever flunks a dissertation defense." Anders held Katherine at arm's length, grinning like a little boy. "They want me to start January third."

"January third," Katherine repeated. She did the math. "That's just three weeks."

"Yeah, isn't that perfect? You can give your notice tomorrow."

All Katherine could think was *No! Wait!* Anders followed her into the kitchen, where he reached for a bottle of merlot. "Celebrate good times," he said, sing-songing the popular tune.

Katherine took down a couple of wine glasses, scrambling to think of something that would make sense to him. "That would only give one week notice, really, since Symbics is closed from Christmas to New Year's. I wouldn't feel right about that—it would be unprofessional." She grasped at a straw, "Have you already accepted the job?"

Anders whipped his hand behind Katherine's head and yanked her hair, forcing her to look up at him. One of the wine glasses shattered on the floor. "Why do you ask," he said.

"Please, Anders, that hurts," she said. The angle of her neck made it hard to talk. He gave her half an inch. "I just assumed we would talk about any job offer you got. Just like we talked before I went with Symbics. I mean, how do you know someplace else wouldn't make a better offer?" Katherine reached back and stroked Anders' hand. "Sweetie, please let go."

Anders maintained his grip. "It's a great job. It's a good salary. It's what I want. Is that going to be a problem?"

Katherine hesitated a fraction too long. Towering above her, Anders' face twisted in rage.

***

A loud knocking on the front door halted Anders' foot in mid air over Katherine's whimpering, curled-up form. She had stopped screaming some time ago, and now simply cowered on the cold linoleum, protecting her face with her arms.

"Sheriff," a man's deep voice announced, followed by more knocking.

Anders stepped smoothly over Katherine, went into the living room, and opened the door. "Yes?" he said. In the kitchen, Katherine scuttled under the kitchen table.

"Good evening, Sir," Katherine heard the deep voice say. "I am Deputy Miller and this is Deputy Hernandez. We received a call about a possible domestic disturbance. May we come in?"

"Of course, Officers. Actually, I am glad you're here. My wife seems to be having some kind of seizure or something." Anders led the officers into the kitchen. "Honey?"

Katherine peered out from under the table. She could only imagine how foolish she looked. "Sorry," she said with a strangled laugh, crawling out and pulling herself up.

The female officer was fortyish and sturdy, with her dark hair pulled back in a bun. She said, "Are you all right, Ma'am?" Katherine gave a sheepish nod and smoothed her hair. But when she went to tuck in her blouse, she winced. Deputy Hernandez said kindly, "Why don't you have a seat, Ma'am."

Katherine saw Deputy Miller's gaze sweep around the kitchen, pausing at the broken wine glass. Stepping between Anders and Katherine, he tilted his head toward the living room. "Sir, how about we go in here."

"But my wife—is she going to be okay? I need to stay with her." Katherine felt Anders' eyes boring into her. She couldn't look at him.

"Sir, Deputy Hernandez is a trained paramedic. Come with me, please."

While the deputy probed her sides with practiced, gentle hands, Katherine listened to Anders' voice in the living room. His measured tones sounded sensible and concerned. He always knew exactly what to do and say. Who would believe her? And if they did believe her, wouldn't they wonder how she could let it happen? No, she had to manage this on her own.

"Do you have a history of seizures?" Deputy Hernandez asked, keeping a comforting hand on Katherine's shoulder.

"No, but I've been getting these headaches," Katherine said. "Sometimes I think I'm going to pass out, I feel so sick. That's probably what happened," she finished lamely, rubbing her temples and a nonexistent headache. Deputy Hernandez looked skeptical. Katherine mustered a smile.

"You may have a cracked rib. I'd like to call an ambulance and have you checked out at the hospital."

"No, no, that's okay, really," Katherine said. The deputy leaned forward a little, her kind eyes giving Katherine a chance to reconsider. "Really, I'll be fine," Katherine insisted.

Finally the deputy reached in her pocket and pulled out a card. She wrote something on it and gave it to Katherine, saying softly, "You have choices, you know." Katherine glanced at the card. It was for the Laurel Center, the local women's shelter, with an 800 number for their Abuse Hotline. Katherine recoiled. *That's not me,* she thought, horrified at the deputy's assumption. The deputy said, still keeping her voice low, "I've written my personal number on the back. We can keep you safe."

Safe. Katherine almost collapsed, sobbing, in the deputy's arms. But she heard Anders in the living room saying firmly,

"Thank you so much, Deputy Miller. I'll keep an eye on her."
Katherine gave Deputy Hernandez a brave smile. "Thanks,"
she said.

The next day, Katherine called in sick and spent all day in
bed. Every ounce of her was hurting, both body and mind.
An unapologetic Anders brought her soup.

Chapter Six

The music that assaulted Katherine's ears when she entered the restaurant with Allen and two others seemed to thump in sync with her throbbing head. *I should have driven over here myself,* she thought, already feeling trapped.

Unsurprisingly, the headache had started in the middle of the night, compounding her aches, but she had hurried to work that morning against Anders' protests. Symbics had become her refuge. Only by convincing Anders that she needed to give her notice in person was she able to escape. Now her head pounded, her side ached, and she felt queasy. Katherine had just taken a prescription pill. It needed to do its job. Fast.

Playa El Toro was a Mexican restaurant by day and a roaring late night bar scene after ten o'clock. This afternoon, the restaurant had closed its shades and lowered the lights in full late-night mode. A huge, U-shaped oak bar divided the room down the middle; behind the bar was a long mirror, illuminated by flashing neon signs that touted Dos Equis and Corona beer. Beer-bottle-shaped blowups with red bows around their necks dangled from the ceiling. To the right of the bar, a disc jockey was stationed at the far corner of a small dance floor, where some folks were already dancing; others had claimed seats in the tables and booths. More booths and tables were on the other side of the bar, along with a table draped with orange and green cloths holding chafing dishes and platters of food. The buffet table was mobbed. Katherine had eaten at the restaurant a couple of times, but she didn't much like spicy food and had had trouble finding anything on the menu that appealed to her. That was another reason she wasn't looking forward to this party.

She turned left and made her way to a booth in the corner, as far from the disc jockey as possible. Jacky Nic was there with Steve, one of his colleagues from the stockroom. Before she could ask, Jacky jumped up and said, "Please, come." He ushered her onto the vinyl bench seat he had just vacated and scooted in next to Steve. "What can I get you?" he said, tilting his bottle of Corona toward her.

"I don't suppose they have Coke?" Katherine said.

"Coming right up," Jacky said. He elbowed through the crowd to the bar. After a few minutes he came back with a red and blue can. "Pepsi okay?" he said.

"Fine, thanks," Katherine said, all but grabbing the soda from his hand. *Caffeine.* She popped the top and took a long swallow, squinting when the cold liquid assaulted the pain behind her eyes. She hoped the chill would soothe the headache, not make it worse.

***

Jacky regarded Katherine. She looked like she was in pain, the way she was scrunching her eyes. *That would be too bad*, he thought. *She is a nice woman.* Before, he used to wonder if Katherine and his Missy could be friends, thinking maybe Katherine could inspire Missy to be more like her. Now, he didn't know. Missy had become withdrawn and lethargic, barely dragging herself out to shop and prepare meals. Jacky knew he was partly to blame; he had withdrawn, too. She had kept a secret from him; a huge secret, and something inside him had changed.

Steve half stood and peered over the back of the booth. "Food table's finally opening up," he said. He gave Jacky's shoulder a rough push. "Come on, man."

They stood and waited for Katherine, but she waved them on. "You go ahead. I'm not really hungry."

***

After Jacky and Steve left, Katherine took another swallow of Pepsi. She wished she had earplugs. Her head hurt. She wanted to be anywhere but here.

Jacky came back with a plate heaped with food in one hand and a bowl in the other. "Quite a spread," he said. "Gotta hand it to Blankenship, he knows how to throw a party."

Katherine glanced at the food and looked away, her stomach rising. *Say something*, she thought. "Yeah, and the best part is he's not here," she said.

"Got that right," Jacky said, tucking into his food.

Katherine looked around. "Where's Steve?"

"On the dance floor. He got to eat half an enchilada, is all."

Katherine tried to smile, but it hurt too much.

Jacky put his fork down. "You okay?"

"Oh, I've just got a headache," Katherine said. "I have some pills but they don't seem to be working."

Jacky pushed his untouched bowl over to her. "Posole Roja. Hot hot—fix you right up. If it doesn't kill you first."

"No, thanks," Katherine said, eyeing the shredded lettuce that was wilting on top. "I'm not much of a fan of Mexican food."

Jacky went to the buffet table and brought back another spoon. "Try it. I'm serious. Missy swears by it."

Dubious, Katherine ate a spoonful of stew. Garlic, pork— spicy, warm. *Not too bad*, she thought. She had another... and then her throat started to burn. Flapping her hand, she croaked, "Water."

Jacky quickly handed her a lime wedge. "Suck on this. I'll be right back."

By the time Jacky returned with a big glass of ice water, Katherine's eyes were streaming. She downed half of the water, then sat back with a gasp. "Lord, Jacky, kill me is right," she said, dabbing her eyes with a napkin.

"I am sorry," Jacky said. "I guess I'm used to it. Truly, I feel terrible."

Hearing Jacky's worried stammer, Katherine shook her head, motioning for him not to feel bad. Then she shook her head again. And again. She looked at him, her eyes wide with amazement. "My headache's better," she said.

Jacky slammed both palms down on the table, making Katherine jump. "*Bon!*" he said. He mock-swiped his hand across his forehead. "Whew."

Steve came back to the booth, swearing he wasn't going to budge until he had eaten. Katherine suddenly felt ravenous. Under Jacky and Steve's tutelage, she worked her way through the buffet, bravely sampling everything and discovering that there were indeed Mexican foods that she liked. She even had a few more spoonfuls of Posole, making sure her water glass was full first, and laughing when Steve scrounged up a bar towel to mop her tears. The more she ate, the better she felt, and she even allowed herself to be enticed onto the dance floor with Allen, Jacky, Steve, and the rest of their gyrating coworkers.

Ouch, she thought as she slid into the booth again. Dancing had been a mistake: her side, knee, and arm were screaming. "Better not," she said in response to Jacky's offer to get her a beer. She pointed at her head, which by some miracle no longer ached, and said, "Prescription meds. Alcohol's a no-no." Overheated, she unbuttoned and shed her sweater, revealing the nubby black shell she wore underneath. Reaching for a menu, she fanned herself.

Jacky slid in across from her. She suspected he was still nursing his first beer, unlike most of their colleagues. He took a sip. "I see you limping?" he asked. "Too much wild dancing—somebody step on your foot?"

"Nah," Katherine said. "I've got a sore... knee. Probably shouldn't have been out there at all."

Jacky was staring at the huge, purple bruise on Katherine's otherwise pale upper arm. Then his gaze shifted to the redness on her other forearm.

"Um," he said, "it's not my place, but how..." He gestured at her bruises.

Katherine glanced where he was pointing and quickly shrugged into her sweater. *Stupid, stupid,* she thought. Laughing lightly, she said, "You should see the other guy." Taking a long drink of Pepsi, she fixed her gaze on the colorful mural on the far wall, willing him to understand that she didn't want to talk about it. She felt him studying her.

Over in the corner, the disk jockey put on a slow song. In the relative quiet, Jacky ventured, "Can I ask you something?" Without waiting for an answer, he said, "Does your husband keep secrets from you? I mean, big secrets?"

Katherine brought her eyes back to Jacky, grateful that he was changing the subject. She remembered the blonde. "Yeah, I'm pretty sure he does." She gave him her full attention. "What makes you ask?"

"My Missy had a big secret. She finally told me, and now it's like this enormous... thing... between us."

Katherine tilted her head with concern, wondering about the details, but not wanting to pry.

Looking down at the table, Jacky continued, "She was with another guy. He beat her and she miscarried."

"Oh, Jacky, how horrible," Katherine exclaimed. "Not while you were married?"

"No, no—before," Jacky said. "We've only been married since March. Hurricane Katrina separated us; I came here and she went to Texas. It happened in Texas." He paused. "I think it's not so much that it happened, but that she didn't tell me. I only found out a few weeks ago. It explained a lot."

"Like what?" Katherine asked, adding, "If I'm not being nosy."

"No, I appreciate you listening, if you don't mind my dumping on you."

Katherine smiled her encouragement. Jacky said, "She won't look for a job, for one. Says she can't bear the way men look at her. She doesn't do much around the house, either. Just sits. She reads, some."

Katherine remembered the cupcakes Missy brought to the company's fall picnic. "Doesn't she cook?"

Jacky smiled. "*Oui*, she does that. She's amazing. But she could do so much more. She's got a degree in medical technology, you know." His voice filled with pride.

Katherine thought, *I should be more like Missy. Anders would like that.*

"So, what are you thinking?" Katherine asked. She had always thought of Jacky as a happy person, and was dismayed to hear the sadness in his lilting voice.

Jacky said, "I think about how to help her. She could maybe take self-defense classes. Work something from home. Get more involved with the church." He thought for a moment. "I wonder why she didn't tell me, and if there are any more secrets. She says she was afraid I wouldn't love her if I knew. I wonder if she's right." His eyes met Katherine's. "It's true that I haven't been able to look at her the same way. But I see her so sad, and I worry is she sorry she married me." Jacky gave a half laugh. "Just like she probably wonders am I sorry I married her."

Jacky fell silent, and Katherine searched for words that might help. Finally she said, "I'm no expert, and probably the last person to give you advice, but it sure sounds to me like you've never stopped loving her. That's why you're so miserable. It sounds like you miss her."

Jacky considered that. "I do. I want my old Missy back."

"Uh uh," Katherine said, shaking her head. "You probably won't get the old Missy back. She's different, and you're different. The question is, can you love the new Missy?"

Jacky leaned back in the booth and ran a finger along the pocked edge of the table. "Let him without sin cast the first stone," he mused. "I need to forgive and forget, don't I." It was more of a statement than a question.

Katherine said, "Maybe not forget, but at least go forward. You know, figure out who you both are now, and go forward together."

The worry lines on Jacky's face began to smooth. Katherine noticed, pleased.

"I was thinking," she said, "that Missy and I need to clone each other."

Jacky straightened. "What do you mean—" But suddenly Katherine gave a little gasp, remembering Anders and her promise that she would give her notice. Today. She glanced at her watch; it was almost four o'clock. "Excuse me a second," she said.

She found Allen at a table next to the dance floor, laughing and waving a mug of beer. His eyes were glazed. "Kat! Join me." When he swept his arm toward an empty chair, beer sloshed out of the mug. "Woop," he said, grinning.

Her resignation would clearly have to wait until Monday. Ditto, she would have to find another ride back to her car.

"No, that's okay, Allen," Katherine said. "I just wanted to tell you what a good time I'm having."

Allen gushed, "It is a good party, isn't it. A great party!" He stood up and staggered onto the dance floor. She hoped someone would call him a cab, later.

Katherine turned away, wondering what on earth she would say to Anders.

Chapter Seven

Jacky watched Katherine make her way back from the other side. Her purposeful stride was gone, replaced by slow, reluctant steps. She hesitated at the restaurant's front door, then surveyed the people in the booths and at the bar. She looked lost.

Jacky hopped out of the booth and went to her. "I'm heading back. Give you a ride?"

"You read my mind," she said gratefully.

As they crossed the parking lot, Jacky said, "A minute ago you said something about wanting to be more like Missy. Were you serious?"

Katherine shrugged. "Oh, it's just that my husband thinks I like my work too much."

"Hey, if you want, I know a few voodoo spells."

Katherine laughed. "I wish it could be that simple."

He unlocked the truck and stood back to let Katherine climb in. But as soon as she stepped onto the running board, her knee gave out. When Jacky grabbed her to keep her from falling, she squealed in pain. "Whoa," she said with a shaky laugh. "Too much dancing."

Jacky froze, letting her steady herself. To ease her embarrassment, he joked, "Can't blame it on drink, unless you get drunk on Pepsi."

Katherine replied with an appreciative, "Hah," and used his proffered arm to lever herself awkwardly into the passenger seat. Her lips were pressed together and she paled with the effort.

By the time he settled into the driver's seat, Jacky had come to a decision. He started the engine, put the truck in gear, and said quietly, "It's not the dancing, is it."

From the corner of his eye he saw Katherine glance at him sharply. He hoped she could see that he wasn't judging, just concerned. He had shared Missy's secret with her—trusted her with a confidence—and he hoped she would trust him, too.

"Mm," she said, noncommittal.

Jacky pressed. "Your husband?"

Katherine kept her tone light. "No secrets from Jacky Nic, eh?"

Jacky's hands tightened on the steering wheel. "Has he always been like this?"

"Oh no," Katherine said. "Just recently. He's been under a lot of stress." She shrugged, and Jacky recognized the same shrug that Missy made, the one that said, "It is what it is, there's nothing anyone can do." Katherine continued, "I'll manage; I'm learning to avoid the triggers."

Jacky opened his mouth, then closed it again. He wanted to find that *salaud* and beat the shit out of him. "He does not deserve you," he said, his voice tight with barely controlled anger.

"That's nice of you to say," Katherine said. "But I owe Anders a lot. I wouldn't be here if it weren't for him."

Jacky scowled. "You might be someplace better if it weren't for him. You ever think about it that way?"

"Huh," she said, as if he'd said something crazy. But after a moment she said, "Huh," again, more softly this time, with a hint of wonder. Then she said, "I keep hoping it's just one of the 'worse' patches in 'for better or for worse'."

"You Catholic?" Jacky asked.

"No, I'm not really anything."

"All right then."

Katherine turned to look at him. "All right then—what?" she said.

Jacky measured his words. "Remember what you said back there, when I said I wanted my old Missy back? These things he—what's your husband's name?"

"Anders."

Jacky repeated, "These things Anders has done to you can't ever be undone. He is different. You are different. The question is, can you love the new Anders?" He spat out her husband's name as if it were a rancid peanut.

Katherine fell silent.

"I'm sorry," Jacky said. "That was way out of line."

"No... no, it wasn't," Katherine said. "It's... you've given me a lot to think about."

A few minutes later, Jacky pulled his truck up next to Katherine's car in the Symbics parking lot. For an awkward moment, neither of them said anything. Katherine put her hand on the door.

Suddenly Jacky touched her elbow. When she turned, he leaned across the seat and kissed her, gently, just brushing her lips with his. They shared sad, half smiles, then Katherine slipped out.

***

Instead of starting the engine and going home, Katherine sat in her car, thinking. She thought about Anders and Symbics; headaches and bruises. She thought about Missy having changed and Jacky wanting to help, in spite of his pain. Several times, she reached for the door handle, then put her hand back in her lap. Finally, she got out of the car and went inside the building, where she found Louisa in her laboratory.

"Kat," Louisa exclaimed, "I thought your Christmas party was this afternoon."

"It was," Katherine said. She hesitated, then took off her sweater, exposing her bruises.

Louisa gasped. "What... how..."

"Anders, two nights ago," Katherine said with a trembling voice. She eased onto a lab stool. "Last month you said something about your spare room?"

"It's yours." Louisa gathered Katherine into a gentle, reassuring hug. "Whatever we can do."

"Thanks, Louisa." Sniffling with gratitude and relief, Katherine rummaged in her purse for a tissue, and came across the card Deputy Hernandez had given her. After blowing her nose, she took a deep breath, then brought out her phone and made the call.

***

Across town, Jacky paused on his front stoop. Studying the Christmas wreath on the front door, he noticed how artfully Missy had arranged the wooden apples, all facing the same direction; their redness highlighted by a shiny red bow and trailing streamers. He fingered the velvet cube in his pocket—after dropping Katherine off he had stopped at Patrick Henry Mall, wanting something, but not knowing exactly what. When the clerk at Boyden Jewelers suggested this, it felt right. Now he wasn't so sure.

When he walked into the house, he found Missy reading on the living room sofa with her feet tucked under her. His heart lurched at the way a lock of her hair curled across her cheek. He could smell something delicious brewing in the kitchen. "That smells *magnifique*," he said. *Too loud, too hearty,* he thought.

When Missy looked up from her book, Jacky saw in her face the same wariness that had been twisting his heart for weeks. She stood up, came over and pecked his cheek—always the dutiful wife—and asked, "How was your day?"

"Fine," he said. Missy turned to go into the kitchen, but Jacky caught her arm. "In fact, better than fine," he said. Missy looked at his hand and Jacky quickly withdrew it. *Idiot. Take it slow. Easy.* He dropped his hand to his side and let her go.

85

Missy's Posole was infinitely better than Playa El Toro's, and even though Jacky wasn't hungry he downed two helpings. He was stalling, he knew. *Just start,* he thought.

"I'm sorry," he said.

"*Pourquoi*—for what?" Missy looked genuinely puzzled.

"For making you so miserable." Jacky held up his hand against Missy's automatic protest. "Bad enough that happened to you, then I make it worse, blaming you for keeping the secret, wanting it to just go away." Jacky struggled to put his thoughts into words. He saw Missy watching him; he couldn't tell what she was thinking. Soldiering on, he said, "We both are wounded by that man, Chérie. It's not you, or me—it is his fault." Missy said nothing. He looked into her eyes, pleading. "I would like to help you heal. You will help me?"

Missy searched his face. Jacky was terrified that she would just shrug, as she had so many times before. But then her eyes filled with tears. She nodded. On shaky legs, Jacky stood up, went to her side, and knelt on one knee. Reaching in his pocket, he brought out the velvet box and gave it to her.

He couldn't remember a word of the speech he had so carefully rehearsed on the way home, so he blurted, "Missy, Chérie, on this new day, going forward, I vow again to love you forever. You will forgive me?"

Missy set the unopened box on the table and threw her arms around Jacky's neck. When she sat back, her face was a sodden mess of streaked makeup, but she was smiling. "I love you, Jacky," she said. "I have never stopped loving you and I never will."

Jacky gestured at the little box. Wide-eyed, Missy opened it. Inside was a braided gold eternity ring, sparkling with diamond chips. He slipped it on her finger, where it would guard her tiny solitaire and wedding band. It fit perfectly.

A Christmas To Always Remember

Narielle Living

Chapter One

A heaviness settled in her, born of the weight of truth, knowledge, and inertia. If she made her move, indulged in her choice, was she risking too much? But if she did nothing, wasn't she risking the same?

The gray edges of her surroundings came into focus as she listened and waited. The house she occupied had clearly undergone many changes through the years, but was still much the same. The hardwood floors were slightly more polished and the walls had an array of colors customized for each room instead of the previous white, but even with the upgrades and decorating it retained the same sense of place, of belonging, of home.

This was where she belonged, but it got so damn lonely that some days she wondered if she would be consumed by the vacuum that had been created within these walls all those years ago.

That wasn't what mattered now, not the gray edges, not the new colors, and not what she knew lurked within this world.

This was a new world she was engaged with, a new way of reaching out to others. She would not hesitate any longer. *I want someone who sees me,* she thought. *I want to be heard. But most of all, I want to be known. Truly known.* Pressing the "add friend" button, a mixture of emotions tumbled through her.

Now, all she had to do was wait and watch.

***

"Hi, my name is Will, and I'm an alcoholic."

The familiar chorus of "Hi, Will!" sounded before quickly settling into silence. Will hesitated, looking out into the crowd. Even after ten years of standing up and telling his story, apprehension set in before he spoke. Fear of judgment mixed with the desire to reach out to others, to help people in the same way he had been helped. Logically, he knew nobody would laugh at him or make fun of him within those walls. But logic had nothing to do with the butterflies doing gymnastics in his stomach.

"I had my first drink when I was twelve years old," he began. "I thought it would be cool to drink the beer my father had bought for a neighborhood picnic, so I snuck one when I knew nobody was paying attention to me." He stopped for a moment, trying to simply tell the story without holding on to the quagmire of emotions that accompanied it. "I didn't have to worry about getting caught. I wasn't a kid anyone paid much attention to anyway." Images of an average looking young teenager filled his mind. "Nothing was wrong with me, but I didn't stand out. I didn't get in trouble, my grades were okay, and I never had a strong opinion. I just didn't get in the way."

Not that there was anything wrong with staying out of trouble, but in a family with five children, his parents had to focus their priorities on putting out whatever fires his siblings had started first. He didn't blame them for overlooking him, and he knew that it was actually a sign of how much they respected him and thought highly of his maturity at that time that they left him to his own devices. It was just too bad that he wasn't able to live up to their expectations.

"I made sure nobody knew I was drinking, even when I became of legal age," he continued. As he spoke, he held onto the same thought he always had when he told his story. *Please, let me help someone tonight. Let my words reach out to those who need it most.*

Inevitably, after he told his story he felt better. Someone usually came up to talk to him, to share their own story with him, to commiserate on shared misadventures. New people approached him, hoping to absorb his sobriety, hoping that they, too, would be able to stop drinking, maybe even for one night.

Being an alcoholic was deadly, for everyone involved.

After the meeting, Will got a cup of coffee at the rickety table leaning in the corner. A small glass bowl with packets of sugar sat next to the powdered milk, the only things that could flavor the not-quite-abysmal coffee. Usually, a tray of store bought cookies sat in the center of the table, and tonight was no exception.

Will stood near the table, Styrofoam cup in hand, glancing around the room. Holding the cup gave him something to do. The chairs had already been put away and people were gathered in groups, talking, or lingering on the edge of the room, wondering if they should talk, or leaving quickly, determined not to be one of them.

Suddenly a man stood before him. Will squinted, wondering how he had appeared. He didn't remember seeing him in the seats, but that didn't mean much. The guy could have been hovering somewhere else, trying not to be noticed.

Will remembered that feeling well, of wanting to fade away and not be seen for who he really was.

Extending his hand, the man said, "Great talk. Very inspiring. My name is Percy."

"Will," he said, shaking the man's hand. "Thanks. I always say a little prayer that my story will reach someone and help them."

Percy smiled. "I'm fairly confident those prayers are always heard." Will stared, wondering about the man in gray that stood before him. Everything about the man was gray, including his hair, his clothing, and… Will squinted again. Yep, even his skin had a grayish tinge to it. *I wonder if he's sick or something. Maybe his liver.*

"I've heard you speak before, but I didn't have time to talk with you," Percy said. "At the meeting over in Gloucester."

"What brings you to Yorktown tonight?"

Percy shrugged, never taking his gaze off of Will. "I felt called to come to this meeting. And I was in town. Hard to ignore that kind of call, right?" When he smiled, Will noticed that the grayness seemed to fade from his eyes, and a sort of light shined through.

"How long have you been in the program?" Will asked. As he spoke with Percy, the room around them faded at the edges. Will was comforted by this man's presence, and a peace descended over him. He knew without having to be told that Percy had been sober for a while.

"I've been working this program for about thirty years," Percy said. "It's changed how I view the world."

Will nodded. "Yeah, me too. Once I sobered up and started looking around me I was amazed at some of the things I heard. I am just so grateful to be given a second chance at my life."

"That's rare," Percy said. "So many don't take the chances offered to them, and so many miss the point of life entirely. But your hard work shows, and you are making a difference. That counts for more than you know." Percy reached into his jacket pocket and pulled out a business card. "I'll be in town for a while. Here's my number, if you ever want to talk or get together. I'm trying to connect with some folks in this area."

Will took the card and looked down at the simple lettering It read: .

> *Percy W.*
> *Consultant*
> *867-5309*

"Really?" he laughed. "You have the same phone number as that song?"

Percy grinned. "You would be amazed at the calls I get. It's rather amusing, actually."

"I'll bet. What kind of consulting do you do?"

"You could say I'm a consultant for a higher power. I do a kind of therapy work." Percy glanced behind him. "I won't take up any more of your time. I think there's someone here who wants to speak with you. Feel free to call me whenever you like. And please don't hesitate to call if you need something."

Will peered over Percy's shoulder, but he didn't see anyone approaching. *He probably wants to talk to others.* "Okay. Nice meeting you, I'll give you a call sometime."

Percy's hand enveloped his again, and a warmth flowed up Will's arm, similar to the feeling he would get when his mother wrapped him in a hug. Peace. Love.

Gotta trust my gut instinct, right? He doesn't seem like a crazy person or serial killer. I can't imagine I'd feel so good about someone who hacked up other people with a kitchen knife… then again, maybe that's how they get away with it…

"Excuse me?" The voice to his left was hesitant and soft, almost as if regretting having spoken. "Do you have a moment?"

Will turned and looked into a pair of haunted blue eyes. "Hi, I'm Will."

"My name is Tessa." She shifted from one foot to the other, eyes glancing over the cookie tray and coffee cups. Her body was tensed and a wariness surrounded her. "The thing is, they told me you could help me. And at this point I'm really hoping that's true."

Chapter Two

Percy hovered behind Dahlia, trying to project an authoritative air. "You don't really have the proper permission for this, you know."

As usual, Dahlia ignored him, fiddling instead with the computer. Percy pressed on. "You cannot forget that you are here for a reason, and you have to focus on the reason. Trying something new like that can have unintended consequences."

For a full minute, only the sound of the ticking clock could be heard. Outside, darkness blanketed the landscape. Somewhere in the distance a car door slammed, and a screech owl hooted a warning. The house waited.

Percy didn't have much time to stand there and try to persuade Dahlia of the error of her ways. "You have a job, and you must stick with it. It's what you chose," he whispered.

Finally, Dahlia turned to him then, her eyes wide. "Yes, I am aware of my choosing. I am aware of every second that the clock ticks off, as I am aware of the swift passing of time while I do what you refer to as my *job*. But really, what else was I to do? Allow—"

"Dahlia, what is wrong?" Percy interrupted. "Why are you now choosing to step outside of everything you know?"

"Is that why you're here? Because I'm stepping outside of things?" Dahlia's mouth quivered as if she would cry, but no tears came. "I know you might not understand this, but I had to do something. I'm so weary of this existence." She stopped, and Percy said nothing, knowing she needed a moment to pull herself together. Finally, her shoulders gave a small heave and she continued. "You don't know what it's like, do you? I want someone who sees me. I want to be heard. But most of all, I want to be known, truly known."

Percy was at a loss. He had been sent without instructions, told to find his way the best he could to help Dahlia and the others through the trying events that were to unfold this holiday season. The problem with that was that he was not told exactly what the trying events were going to be, so he was left guessing about an unknown future. "I don't know that this Facebook thing is exactly the way to be seen or heard," he began.

"But I can use it, it's here for me," Dahlia said. "It's easy to use, and I can reach out to others with this tool."

Percy kept quiet. There was nothing he could say, really. He knew every action had a consequence, and Dahlia had started down a path that might have serious consequences. He also knew that when it came to choices, some were not his to make.

Headlights shined on the wall as a car pulled into the driveway. "I cannot stay," Percy said. "But remember, whatever you do, be careful. It's not just you that could get hurt."

***

Will pulled into the driveway and checked his rearview mirror one more time. Sure enough, the car was still behind him. After speaking with Tessa, then his sponsor, Rick C., he didn't question anything, he simply let go. Some things in life were meant to be, and he believed that being asked to speak that night was no coincidence.

According to his sponsor, as Will told his story at the meeting, Rick had thought about Will's house. He told Will it was ideal for Tessa since there was an unused apartment built over the detached garage. It had been so long since anyone had lived there that Will never thought about it until he needed the space. He generally didn't lease it out in case one of his family members visited or someone needed a place to stay. Besides, he liked having the privacy and the house all to himself. Not that someone living over the garage would get in the way, but it was another person on his property. This could mean he would occasionally be required to come out of his shell and communicate in some way, and it might even happen before he'd had his morning coffee.

I didn't really need to take that stupid online test to know I'm an introvert. Hell, everyone who knows me knows that.

Tessa had pulled her car into the parking space next to him in the driveway. She sat, apparently waiting for him, probably not wanting to cause trouble. The impression he'd gotten of her was that she wanted to fade away, to be invisible, and not disturb anyone. Her manner suggested a woman not expecting much from anyone and perched to bolt if necessary.

He would not have considered renting his apartment to her if his sponsor hadn't pressed him on the matter. "I can tell you she needs a place to stay, like right now," Rick had said. "Tonight. And I can also tell you she's good for the money. In fact, if she doesn't pay, I'll pay her rent for her. But I can't tell you anything more than that, other than she came to us through other friends in other groups. Can you do this?"

"I'm not worried about the money," Will said. And he wasn't, since he didn't have a big mortgage. He'd bought the house when he'd first gotten sober, and it had been as much of a mess as he was. Because of the disrepair of the house, it was dirt cheap. The first time he'd seen it he'd wanted to cry. The exterior paint was a dirty, faded yellow and peeling from the clapboard, and the center of the home looked as if it were sagging. The inside of the home smelled like grease, mold, and small, dead animals. Parts of the ceiling had collapsed, and Will was careful where he stepped in case the flooring gave way.

"You could only get a rehab loan for this," the Realtor had said with disdain. "I wouldn't go upstairs if I were you, it doesn't look safe. Are you ready to look at the next one?"

"No." Will wasn't ready to look at anything else, because he'd taken one look at the falling down death trap and knew he had to save it. As he stood, quietly assessing what needed to be done, he could swear the house took a deep, raspy breath, as if it were recovering from emphysema. A ray of sunlight slanted through the window, illuminating worn, olive green carpeting. Parts of the kitchen and bathroom had been torn apart, and clearly nothing worked. Built in 1913, the old farmhouse sat on eight acres in Seaford, Virginia. Maybe it was the age of the home, or maybe something in him was responding to the obvious disrepair, but the odd thing was, he felt good here. He felt safe. He felt protected.

Over the years he'd put savings and sweat equity in and remodeled the place so it became an aesthetic haven for him. He wanted a home, not just a pile of wood and wires, and that is exactly what he worked so hard to achieve. Home.

And maybe now he could provide someone else with the same sense of place, a home where she could feel safe. Because Will was pretty sure that at that moment Tessa felt anything but safe. She remained huddled in her car, as if waiting for him to give her a signal that she could exit.

He smiled at her, hoping to be encouraging. Instead, she shrank back in her seat. *Okay, maybe the smile made me look like a homicidal maniac. Or maybe she wants to stay far away from me.*

Something about Tessa inspired a protective feeling in him, made him want to stand in front of her and defend her with everything he had. Maybe it was the cautious way she held herself, or how she used her long hair to shield her face when she was talking with him. She was pretty, but he also thought she was a bit too thin. *I should have her over for dinner once in a while, try to get her to eat some hearty meals. It looks like she hasn't been eating much for a while.*

Not sure what to do, or how to coax her out of the car, he decided to be direct. "Do you want to see the apartment?" he yelled, as if she were deaf. She nodded and opened her door, but still didn't step out.

"It's empty right now, but it does have furniture," he continued in the same tone of voice.

"Why are you yelling?" she asked.

"I don't know," he said. "You weren't getting out of the car and I didn't know what to do."

"I wasn't sure what you wanted me to do," she said.

That was an unusual thing to say, but Will was trying not to judge her. Clearly she was working through some emotional debris, but at that moment he was focused on getting her to look at what he hoped would become her new home.

Always trying to save someone or something.

"The stairs are on the side of the garage," he said. "Right this way." And as if she were a stray cat that didn't quite trust humans, she cautiously followed his lead.

One step at a time.

***

Tessa wasn't quite sure how to act around Will. She knew he was trying to be nice, but she couldn't stop herself from wondering when he'd change, when he'd start asking for something she didn't want to give. *Are people really this nice? Who the hell is this guy?*

She glanced over at the main house as she climbed the stairs behind him, careful to maintain a good distance so he couldn't reach her if he turned around. She still didn't know who to trust, and she knew that carelessness could cost her her life. But all the self-help books she'd immersed herself in encouraged her to find her inner strength, trust the path before her, and know that all would be well. Easy enough for those who've only dealt with… normal bad times. But no, she couldn't let herself wallow in the past. The future was in front of her, beckoning like a potential friend asking her in for coffee. She could only move forward, and trust that her instincts—and common sense—would guide her.

The front porch to the farmhouse next to the garage was illuminated, and a light was on inside, too. A large elm stood in the front yard, probably providing shade during the height of summer. Crickets sang their chorus, and no traffic could be heard. The house looked warm, inviting... it looked like home. A shudder rippled through her at the thought of home, and she had to force herself to look away. She had to be careful, it might not be good to want too much.

She was grateful for the light illuminating the staircase, and she was also glad that Will simply opened the door and stepped inside. She didn't want to stand too close to him on that little landing at the top of the steps. *Stop it*, she scolded herself. *He's probably just a really nice guy. Not everybody is... bad.*

He had already walked to the other side of the kitchen when she stepped inside.

"As Rick told you, the place is fully furnished and the kitchen is stocked with everything you'll need to cook, but there is no food," Will said. "There are some dry goods, essentials like coffee, but you'll need to make a run to the grocery store. They might still be open if you need something right now."

Her mind was blank as she walked through the space, dazed. The rooms were simple, with neutral colors on the walls and furniture that looked almost new. The scent of cleaner filled the air, as if someone had been expecting her and gotten the place ready.

Tears filled her eyes before she could grab control of her emotions. "Thank you," she said. "I don't know how much you want in rent—"

"One thing at a time," he said. "First, let's sit down and talk. If you want, I can make a pot of coffee."

She shook her head, her stomach sinking at his words. Talk. Whenever someone wanted to talk to her that meant something was coming. Usually it wasn't something good. Although talking was supposed to be a good thing, supposed to clear the air. The books she'd read said that communication was important. *I guess it depends on who you are communicating with.*

She took a breath. She had no choice right now, she had to trust this guy. At least his eyes were kind—without pity when he spoke to her. But once he found out her history he would probably fall all over himself with the pity thing. Or he'd run away. Or his dark side would come out. Or… Suddenly, she heard the silence in the room. Apparently he had been talking, and now he wasn't. He was waiting for her to comment on whatever he had said.

"Okay," she said. *Keep it vague, he'll never know I wasn't listening.*

"You didn't hear anything I said, did you?" His words were softened by his smile, and the knot in her stomach released.

"Sorry," she said. "I was lost in my thoughts… the space is amazing. The energy here… it feels safe. I don't know how else to describe it."

Will nodded. "That's the exact thought I had the first time I saw the house. It was falling apart, a real mess. But I knew it had good bones. I believe that if you look hard enough, you can spot the light shining within anything."

Tessa smiled, her first real smile in a long time. Will hadn't said anything profound, but he'd put her at ease and made her think that maybe, just maybe, everything would be okay.

Chapter Three

Will eased onto the couch with his laptop balanced in one hand and a bowl of popcorn in the other. This was his time to relax, scroll through his email, check Facebook, and watch TV. Simple. Nothing taxing, nothing he had to think about. Tessa was settled safely in the apartment, and he had left her with his phone number in case she needed anything. He flipped through the cable guide, trying to find something good, and settled on a crime show. Opening his laptop, he first checked his email, deleting most of them. Then, he opened his Facebook account. He'd been scrolling for a few minutes, alternating his attention between the television show where an entire family was gathered for Sunday dinner to reading his friends' updates. After a moment, he noticed he had a friend request.

Dahlia Faith Warren. He frowned for a moment, not certain he knew her despite her profile saying she lived in Yorktown. Her profile picture showed a picture of an old fashioned Singer sewing machine. He clicked over to her timeline, where she actively engaged in conversations with others. *Okay, so she's a real person.* He clicked "Accept Friend Request" and typed in a message on her timeline. "Thanks for the friend request, nice to meet you." He always tried to be polite in his online interactions, especially since noticing that so many lacked social niceties that they might have in a face-to-face conversation.

A blast of heat kicked on as the house shuddered around him. *Damn, I've lost track of time. It's late November already, I'm going to have to get the furnace serviced soon for the winter.*

He was curious about his new friend Dahlia and started clicking through her pictures and information. She had lots of pictures on her profile, but unfortunately none of them were of people. She had plenty of memes and pictures of animals, mostly cats, but he couldn't find any photos of her. *That's kind of strange.* Curious now, he sent her a private message.

Hi Dahlia,

Thanks for reaching out with a friend request. I see that you live in Yorktown. I'm in Seaford. Maybe we've crossed paths before?

Will

Closing his computer, he settled in to watch the rest of the show and finish his popcorn. If he didn't hear back from Dahlia, he would unfriend her. After all, you never really knew who was behind a profile picture.

***

Dahlia knew he was there before he said anything, but she wanted to finish typing her answer to Will.

Hi Will,

I don't think we've ever met in person, but I've been in this area for a very long time. Thanks for accepting my request. How do you like living in Seaford? I love this area!

Dahlia

"What in tarnation are you doing?" Percy whispered in a loud voice.

"Shh, you're going to wake Will. He's a light sleeper, you know."

Percy paced behind her, his steps light but clearly agitated. "So, let me get this straight. You have a job to do: protect this house and all who live in it. Yet, here you are, contacting the person who lives here, engaging in some type of conversation, and using his computer to do it... does that cover it?"

"Yes, Percy, I believe that covers it. But you don't understand—"

"What I understand is that you are putting your position in jeopardy as well as possibly causing harm to those you have chosen to protect. This cannot go on."

"But—"

"You know who, and what, we are. We are the ones who stay, the ones who have died but do not cross over. You are spirit, you are not flesh—"

"Others can see us, sometimes. They see you—"

"When we choose to let them see us, yes. But let me remind you: we are the gray ones, the ones whose lives slipped by without purpose, without grabbing hold of what we needed to do to fully appreciate who we could become. You are here to not only grow your own soul but to help others in their journey through this realm."

"That's not fair." Anxiety and despair washed through Dahlia. "I was murdered. I never got the chance to live up to my purpose, or grow into who I needed to become. Killed by a darkness so evil that I never stood a chance. And now, I am left here to defend others when it chooses to invade again."

Percy grew quiet for a moment before speaking. "This was your choice. You wanted to stay. Are you choosing otherwise now?"

The night air grew still, and the house itself seemed poised to hear her answer. *Even in this non-physical state, I have fanciful thoughts.* But it was clearly time for her to confess what had been happening.

"Percy, I… I do not understand why I am having these feelings. Since 1926 I have been here, guarding this house, even during those times it was empty. Always, I have felt that I belonged. But now I am restless, and that makes no sense to me. How can I be restless when I do not have a body? How can I want things that I did not even care for when I was alive?"

She paced around the room, dismayed at the emotions that crashed through her. "What is happening to me?" she whispered.

Percy stepped in front of her and waited to speak until she looked up at him. "I have never seen this before, but you are in a unique situation. Most of the time we are sent to help specific souls through a life event. You, however, have been named sentry of this place, asked to stand guard and wait to dispel evil that might enter. How many times have you been called upon to do so?"

Dahlia didn't have to think about it; each instance of evil entering was seared into her mind. "Many. They came, the dark ones, for whatever reason. I did what I could to banish them. The first time was the hardest. I wasn't sure what to do, but I had to do something."

"What happened that first time?" Percy asked.

Dahlia knew Percy was humoring her, trying to get her to talk, but she answered anyway. Maybe he could help her navigate this distressing situation. "The people who moved into the farmhouse after... after my death, they were distant relatives. Cousins, maybe. I believe they came because they were all the family that was left, so they must have inherited the place. When they first moved in, I was new to this, and not entirely certain of my role..." Dahlia stopped as the memories came to her, a series of pictures imprinted from so long ago. "It took me a while to realize what the father was doing to his daughter. Then, when I finally understood what was happening, I pushed him out."

"What do you mean, pushed him out?" Percy said.

"I'm not certain how I did it, but I just sort of—pushed, with my mind, I think. Then one day he decided to leave, and he never came back. It was the best thing for that young girl, really. Once he left them, the mother was so angry with him about his desertion that she probably wouldn't have taken him back if he'd tried."

Dahlia thought about all the times she'd pushed evil away from the house, from the land. All the times she'd followed her purpose. "So many people," she said. "I remember the other killers, not the one who killed me, but the ones who were passing through. Montie Rissell... James Gallagher... Swannie LeMont..."

Percy cocked his head at her. "I know the first name, but I am not familiar with the others. Did they, too, kill?"

Dahlia nodded. "Not here, though, never here. Yes, Montie is still in jail, but the others, they were never caught. I believe the newspapers had names for them, but nobody ever traced them to the killings. But I knew, I could see it around them. So I pushed them away."

"And during that time, did you feel the way you do now?"

"No, that's the strange part." Dahlia started pacing again. "I was very content to know that I was keeping this place safe to be a real home, that I was not allowing the darkness entry to this space. I was doing my job. But little by little I watched people leave, families moving away or people dying, and everything around changing so much. Nobody could see me, I made sure of that. I didn't want the house to get a reputation as haunted; you know how people can talk. Then, for some reason, I wished to be a part of it, to be heard. For heaven's sakes, I once fantasized about Will asking my opinion on what color to paint the walls. What is happening to me?"

"I don't know," Percy said. "But I'll do my best to find out."

***

Will held a cup of coffee in one hand and tucked a container of French vanilla creamer in the other. He gently knocked on the door and stepped back, knowing Tessa would be freaked out if he stood too close. When she came to the door, she looked exhausted. Her hair was a tangled mess, as if she'd been running her hand through it, and she had dark circles under her eyes. He tried not to let his surprise show.

"I brought you a cup of coffee to start the morning," he said, holding up the cup. "I don't know what you take in it, but I've got creamer." He stopped talking and waited while she stood before him. Finally, she stepped away from the entry and gestured for him to come in.

"Thank you," she said in a careful tone.

Enough was enough. He couldn't stand seeing her like this. Whatever had happened, she had to know she was safe here. "Listen, I've got to go to work in a little while. I'll leave you my cell phone number in case you need anything. But, seriously, you've got to level with me. Right now you look like crap, like you didn't sleep at all last night. What's going on?"

He knew his approach might be too direct, but he wasn't about to just stand by while someone looked constantly afraid.

She sighed and walked to the kitchen counter, leaning against it as if for support. "I stayed up all night watching the front street. I thought someone was out there."

Will was instantly alert. "Tell me about what you saw."

"A car, parked on the road. Sometime around two a.m. something woke me, and I got up and looked outside. I thought I saw a light on in your house, downstairs, then I noticed a car driving slowly down the street."

I don't leave any lights on at night, Will thought. *Maybe she saw a reflection from a mirror or something.* "Go on," he urged.

"Something about the way the car was driving creeped me out, then it stopped." She closed her eyes for a moment and took a deep breath. "When the car stopped and the headlights went out, I knew it was here to watch this place. It stayed out front until dawn."

Will held up a hand to stop her. "Okay, hold on for just a minute, I need to make a call." He pulled out his cell phone and called the office. "Hey, Mikey, it's Will. Listen, I don't have any interviews lined up this morning, but I wanted to let you know I might be a little bit late coming in. No, everything's fine, I just have to take care of something here. Right. Thanks." Disconnecting, he looked into Tessa's eyes.

"If you believe you were in some kind of danger, it's time for you to tell me what's going on." A look of fear defined her face. "Tessa, listen to me. I don't care what brought you here. I've done things in my life that I don't like people knowing about. I've lied, cheated, stolen, you name it. But if there is a problem then you need to tell me about it. I'm not going to judge you, but I can't help you if I don't know what's going on."

She didn't move, didn't speak. He crossed the room, went to the living room, and sat on the couch. "I'm a reporter, my job is getting information from people. I'm not leaving until you tell me." He knew it was a risk to push her like this, but if she'd been up all night thinking she was in danger then he didn't have the luxury of waiting for her to open up.

Tears began to roll down her cheeks. "I can't," she whispered. "What if I tell you, and..."

"What if you don't tell me and something worse happens?" Will said. "Obviously you're being protected by people in AA, because that's how you got to me. Now all you have to do is tell me what's going on."

After a moment, Tessa straightened and faced him. "What's the worst thing you've ever done?"

Will didn't even have to think about it. "It's kind of a toss-up between a few things. Take your pick of which is the worst." He smiled sadly. "First, I stole my grandmother's engagement ring to buy drugs. I did this the day of my grandfather's funeral, when nobody was in the house." Her eyes widened a bit, and he went on. "Or maybe it was the time I had sex with a person who was not my girlfriend. This was a couple of hours after I had driven drunk and wrecked the car, sending my girlfriend to the hospital." She looked even more surprised, which was good. Maybe this would help her open up. "And if you were listening to my story the other night, you'd know the part about stealing my parents' credit card numbers so I could do whatever it was I thought I was going to do." He waved his hand in the air. "So, take your pick of what was the worst thing, I've done them all. And I thank God that I'm sober now, that I don't do that same kind of stupid crap that hurt so many people just so I could get my stupid fix. I'm grateful that's all over. Your turn."

She hung her head and spoke so softly he had to strain to hear her. "I sold myself."

"For drugs?"

When she shook her head no, he was confused. "You're talking about sex, right?"

She nodded. "I did it because I had to."

He waited a moment, and when she didn't add anything, he stopped himself from questioning her. Her hands were shaking, and a nasty suspicion was taking root in his mind.

"I was sixteen years old when I was first approached by someone I thought was a friend," she said. "At least, I wanted him to be a friend. He was really cute, and I was not a popular kid. But he was interested in me, and he was always there."

"How old was this guy?" Will asked.

She shrugged. "He said he was eighteen. I don't know if it was true or not, because I found out later that he was a scout."

Will was confused. "A boy scout?"

A faint smile crossed Tessa's face, the first he'd seen all morning. "No, he was a scout for another person. His job was to find kids like me and lure me to his boss."

Will had never heard of this before. "What do you mean, kids like you?"

Tessa's faint smile was replaced by a grimace, as if she were in pain. "I was an awkward kid, shy and not really pretty at all. Plus, I was in the foster care system, and at that time I was on my tenth or eleventh placement, I can't remember. Maybe it was twelve, who knows."

Will was stunned. "Wait a minute, do you mean that you lived in more than ten foster homes?"

Tessa nodded. "Yes. I guess I was difficult to place, but I'm not sure why. I'd be living somewhere then the next thing I knew the social worker would show up and tell me it was time to go."

He was having trouble imagining what this would be like for her as a young kid. Definitely not a traditional childhood, that's for sure. "Was this here, in Virginia?"

She shook her head. "No, in Florida. They weren't very good at checking up on me, and I only saw the worker when it was time to move. So when this boy, who said his name was Joey, asked me to run away with him, it seemed like a good idea at the time. It's not like I had any family that cared, anyway. I left a note for the family and hopped in the car with Joey."

"But it wasn't what you thought," Will said.

"Not even a little bit." Tessa stopped talking again and began to pace. Then she stopped, and as if making up her mind, looked Will directly in the eye. "Joey took me to the guy he worked for, who for the past decade has kept me as his worker. I was fed and given a place to stay, but I had to have sex with the men he arranged. At first, I wouldn't do it, but..." Her voice trailed off as her face took on a faraway look. "This guy, he knew what he was doing..."

Will almost hated to know, but if he was going to help her in any way, he had to get the information. "What could be worse than being forced to have sex with strangers?"

Tessa shook her head, as if wondering how Will had become so naïve. *I'm kind of wondering the same thing. How did I not know about this? How the hell did this girl survive any of that?*

"In the beginning, he must have known how I'd act. I wasn't the only girl, and he'd built quite the business. So, he bought me a puppy. A little golden retriever, a sweet little baby. And whenever I'd refuse to do what he told me to do, he wouldn't say anything, but he would hurt the puppy." She paused and took another breath, as if trying to control her emotions. "I tried not to care, but I couldn't stand that I was the reason for all the yelping and crying. He hurt my dog, so I felt like I had no choice. I know how stupid that sounds—"

"Actually, it sounds brave," Will said. "Anybody that would sacrifice themselves to help an innocent animal is more than a decent human being. You're a hero."

Tessa actually laughed then. "I think you're being a little dramatic."

"Compared to what I've done in my life? No, I don't think so. I'm assuming you ended up in AA after you got away from this guy?" He knew he was taking a chance asking, but he'd come this far in her story, so he might as well hear the whole thing.

"Yes. Brian—that's the guy that was in charge of me—would give me something to drink, usually vodka, before he'd send me out. Said it would loosen me up, make me more fun. Pretty soon I needed it just to get through my days. I tried to tell him I didn't want any, but he didn't care about that. He poured it down my throat. Literally. So once I... got away, I tried not to drink. But I needed help, so I started going to meetings."

Will stood, walked back to the kitchen, and peered through the blinds at the street outside. He knew that the next part of the conversation was the important part, so he didn't want to rush her. Hopefully his face betrayed nothing, but anger roiled his stomach. People who trapped others into those types of situations were evil, pure and simple. Although he'd had many conversations with friends about truth, goodness, and evil in this world, there was no question about this. Darkness had invaded Tessa's life, and he knew he would do whatever he needed to do to keep it at bay. Permanently.

He waited a minute, then asked, "How did you get away?"

"Luck," Tessa said. "And books." Will raised his eyebrows at her, not sure he'd heard her correctly. She stood straighter, as if thinking about books gave her courage. "He had this one customer that I had to meet at the library. A regular. Sometimes I had to wait for him, and sometimes he wouldn't show up. There wasn't much I could do; Brian was always watching me, so I told him that I needed to look like I was there for a reason. I would take books off of shelves and start reading. I tried reading lots of different kinds of books: mysteries, teen, non-fiction, but the ones I liked the best were the self-help books."

Will's respect for Tessa grew. Here was a woman who had endured pain of all kinds, who was truly able to help herself and get out of a terrible situation.

"After a while, I realized all the books had the same theme," she continued. "I had the power to free myself, the ability to make my life what I wanted it to be. So one day, I did the unthinkable. I tore a page out of a book, angled myself so nobody could see what I was doing and wrote a note in the book. Then I approached the librarian. Brian was watching, but I was very careful. All he heard me say was that I was reporting a vandalized book. Two days later the detectives were there, waiting for me. It all happened so quietly, I was amazed. All this time I'd been living with this monster, then one day it just ended."

But Will knew better. He knew what it meant that someone was watching the place all night. "It hasn't ended, though, has it?"

She shook her head, tears threatening to spill yet again. "No, it hasn't."

Chapter Four

The late afternoon sun warmed the front room of the farmhouse, dancing off of the gleaming mahogany sideboard and settling in as the clock ticked comfortably. Dahlia wandered through the rooms, once again enjoying what Will had done to the house. *He has a wonderful eye*, she thought. *He's made it into a real home, brought a sense of peace to this place.*

Still, something was bothering her. A feeling of disquiet shivered through her, the sense that the energy around her was off. *It's almost as if I'm waiting for something bad to happen. I hope not…* She thought about the new tenant over the garage, Tessa. Dahlia had seen her the few times she'd been over, and she wondered what was simmering between Tessa and Will. Tension often lined Tessa's face, and Will acted as her protector, even in his own home. She knew Tessa had faced something terrible and survived, and she admired the woman greatly for this. *Perhaps this has something to do with what she's been through.*

Dahlia wandered into the front hallway and stood before the mirror that hung over the antique regency console table. She stared for a moment, then decided to do it. *Why not? If I want to be seen, then I have to be able to let people see me.*

Dahlia hadn't spent much time trying to appear to people, since her primary focus at the house was keeping evil at bay. It had never occurred to her that she should appear, ever. But things were changing, and as she had said to Percy she wasn't sure why she was having these feelings. All she knew was that she felt more compelled than ever to try to appear.

Right now, she thought. *It's as good a time as any.*

Focusing, she closed her eyes. She wasn't exactly certain how this worked, but she began with the idea that she could be seen. *I am present, I am visible...*

She slowly opened her eyes and smiled. Her reflection in the mirror smiled back at her. Maybe this wouldn't be too difficult after all.

"What the hell are you doing in my house?" The voice made her jump.

"Will?" she said.

"How do you know my name? And answer my question: what the hell are you doing here?"

She wasn't sure how to answer. This had never happened to her before, and she didn't know what to do. She might be dead, but that didn't stop the nauseous feeling that swept through her.

"Listen, it's not what you think," she began. "I have a reason for being here—"

"Start with your name. I want to know your name, right now." His face was thunderous, and he loomed over her. If she didn't know better she might have thought he would hurt her, but this was Will. He wouldn't hurt anybody, not intentionally.

But he could see her. He could absolutely see her. Only this probably wasn't the best time for that to happen, as much as she'd wanted it. She had no choice but to answer him.

"I'm Dahlia," she whispered. "Dahlia Faith Warren." His silence was like a storm, with dark emotions reaching out and swirling all around the room. *Does he even remember how he knows me?*

"What?" he exploded. "The girl from Facebook?"

When she nodded, his face got red. "I don't know what your story is, or what kind of game you're playing, but this is as far as it goes. We're done here. You need to leave, now."

She felt the energy start to siphon out of her. "You-you're telling me to go? From this house?"

"Right now. And don't come back."

"But, you don't understand—" It was too late. He'd already turned his back on her, and didn't see her fade away to nothingness after banishing her from the place she had sworn to protect.

***

Percy stepped into the valley, uncertain about what had happened. Large rock formations rose up around him, dark figures that were almost menacing. The light was gray, creating a grim color palette in the barren landscape. Dahlia sat in the center of the valley with her arms wrapped around her bent legs and her head resting on her knees. She must have heard him approach, because she spoke without looking at him. "I have failed."

He waited a moment before answering. This was going to be tricky, he knew, and his answer must somehow sustain her for what might possibly come. "There are always many different outcomes to any situation. We don't yet know what will happen."

She looked at him then, empty and void of emotion. Percy didn't know what to make of this being in front of him. He'd never known Dahlia to be so... hollow, even after she'd been murdered.

"Do you remember?" she asked. "A long time ago, but not really. 1926."

Confusion laced his thoughts as he tried to figure out what she meant. "Remember?"

Then, as if she had sent him a vision, he could see it. The scene before him played out with an excruciating inevitability; something he was powerless to not see.

The blinding blue sky wrapped the lilac-scented world. A soft, early summer wind blew, and at first only silence reigned. Then, the noises began to intrude. The buzzing of cicadas. Birdsong punctuating the breeze. Crisp shadows indicating the late afternoon. And the gentle humming from a woman hanging laundry on the clothesline behind the farmhouse.

The woman outside was the only person evident at the cheery yellow farmhouse. In the distance, a low rumbling came from a cloud of dust. She looked up and smiled at the sight. By the time the car had parked in the front driveway, she had put down her clothes and rushed out to greet him.

But her smile faded as he strode toward her. Panic replaced delight, and she turned to run, a fruitless endeavor. He caught her easily, grabbed her long hair, and pulled her head back. He then shoved a knife into her abdomen and dragged her around the house to the entry of the basement.

The vision cleared. Percy was once again alone with Dahlia in a dark, barren world. "His name was Charles. He was my husband, you know. He got away somehow. But once I realized I was dead, that my life had been stolen from me, I made the decision that I would never again allow that kind of evil to creep back. I would stand with the light and not allow the darkness in. I made a promise, one that I can no longer keep."

She looked at Percy then, still blank. "What is to happen to me now?"

"I don't know," he said. "But I'm going to do everything I can to help you."

"And Will," she added. "Because I think he's going to need it. I don't know how I know this, but the darkness is returning. And this one feels the same."

"What do you mean?"

Dahlia did not hesitate to answer. "This one feels just like the other evil. The one that killed me the first time."

Chapter Five

Tessa put her hand on Will's arm in an effort to comfort him. He appreciated her concern, but at that moment her touch was somewhat distracting. But he did nothing to remove her hand, as he knew that even that slight show of caring was an effort for her. She'd come a long way in recovering from being a sex trafficking victim, but some things were still difficult, like getting close to people.

"How did she get in?" Tessa asked.

Will shook his head. Never mind how did she get in, how did she leave? He had turned his back on his unwanted guest and she simply vanished, as if she had never been there.

"This whole thing is just really strange," he said. "I don't know, it feels off somehow. I can't really explain why, it just…"

"Having someone come into your house is going to leave you feeling violated," Tessa said. "It's kind of a weird thing to do."

Will agreed. "But there's more to it than that." He hesitated, wondering how much to tell her. "I'm going to tell you something, but you have to promise me that you won't get weirded out or think I'm insane or need to see a psychiatrist." Tessa stiffened beside him, so he hurried to add, "It's about Dahlia."

She looked at him, concern evident in her eyes. "I promise to *try* not to think you're crazy."

"Try?"

She laughed and shook her head. "C'mon, that's the best you're going to get without me knowing what you're going to say."

"Then I guess I'll have to take it." He took a deep breath before continuing. "The thing is, I keep feeling like I've made a mistake."

"You think kicking out a complete stranger who broke into your house is a mistake?"

"No, that's not what I meant. I don't think she's a complete stranger." *This is where it's going to get weird*, he thought. *But I've got to say it to someone.* "Listen, Tessa, I trust you. And I know how this is going to sound, so I'm going to take a chance and say it. To you. But probably nobody else, okay?" After Tessa nodded, he continued. "When I walked in and saw Dahlia standing there, I knew who she was."

"Because she lives in the area," Tessa said. "You've seen her around here before?"

Will shook his head. "No, I've never seen her outside of this house. But... I've seen her before. Here."

"I don't understand," Tessa said. "She's broken in before? When?"

"I'm not sure she broke in, exactly. The thing is, I've caught glimpses of her in weird places, but I thought I was dreaming or seeing things. And each time I've seen her it's been as if she was not quite clear, like I was seeing her in a fog or something, and it's always been really fast then she disappeared. Or I would catch a glimpse of her in a mirror, then she was gone. But not like a real person was here, more like a..."

"A ghost?" Tessa offered.

Will didn't want to look at her then. Instead, he focused on trying to push his inexplicable sadness away. "I suppose you could say that."

The house no longer felt like a home. Instead, it felt empty, and the feeling that he'd gotten when he'd first seen the place was no longer there. Not only that, it didn't feel safe, but he didn't know if that was because he was worried that someone was watching Tessa.

"Listen," Tessa said, moving to sit in front of Will so he could see her face. "I don't think you're crazy. I think you've probably seen someone, or something, here, and maybe this person looked like the woman who came in. Maybe she's even a relative or something. But here's the thing: you're not going to be happy until you figure this out. So why don't you try to contact her, talk to her, and see what she wanted? Obviously you didn't get a chance to talk when you saw her, so maybe you can find her and ask her some questions."

A flash of hope pierced his inertia. "You're right, that's exactly what I should do. Thank you."

She stood, pulling him up with her. "It's always easier to help other people figure out what to do instead of yourself.

C'mon, let's get to the AA meeting. I think being with your sponsor and friends will make you feel better, too."

He held her hand as they left, in a friendly gesture more than anything else. But it felt right to do that, it felt right to be next to her and talking about life, leaving to go somewhere together. "It's Christmas eve tomorrow," he said. "When was the last time you celebrated the holidays?"

He thought he knew the answer, but once again, Tessa surprised him. "I celebrated it every year. I would find a way to give thanks, to say a prayer to the Great Spirit or the little baby Jesus, who I imagined as looking very different than the pictures they try to shove at us, and I would try to sneak a piece of greenery into a fire or breathe in goodness or just offer up general thanks for being alive."

"Really?" He tried to imagine what it would have been like for her, but he couldn't. He simply could not picture the scene she had just painted, and it angered him that she had been forced to endure the pain of that type of slavery.

"I remember reading in one of those books how important gratitude is, no matter what. I'd made up my mind that my life would not continue to be what it was. I didn't know how and I didn't know when, but I knew I'd get out sooner or later. Besides, having an internal Christmas celebration was the best way to say F-you to the man who tried to control me."

As they walked out the door and he locked it behind him, Will marveled at Tessa's ability to adapt to a life not at all of her choosing. Plus, she was insightful and kind, a combination that intrigued and attracted him. *Slow down, boy, she's just come off a really bad experience. You can't mess things up for her.*

At the very least he could protect her. Because as he pulled out of the driveway with her in the passenger seat, he saw the SUV parked down the street. And he knew, without having to be told, that whoever was in it was waiting for her.

Let them come, he thought. *Let them try to get through me and my friends and hurt her.*

He was ready.

***

The weather had grown colder, and a damp chill permeated the air. Christmas decorations punctuated the area; wreaths on doors, light-up reindeer on lawns, and Christmas trees outlined in picture windows. Percy stood outside the church, waiting for Will. He greeted everyone who walked past him to go to the AA meeting, smiling and sending positive thoughts at those who were there to heal. *What is this situation going to do to Will's sobriety?* This was the first time that thought had occurred to Percy, but he pushed the question away. Percy knew that everything unfolded in its own time, and he simply had to trust the process and believe that all would work out for the best. Besides, Will had been in constant contact with his sponsor and a multitude of others from the program lately. *He's been so busy talking with the others that he really hasn't even had a moment to spare,* Percy thought. *He's not answering his phone, either. And it's not like I can just show up at his house. This is too important.*

Percy knew he had to find a way to talk face-to-face with Will tonight. He couldn't take the chance that Will would be distracted or not hear him. Plus, mixed in with all the canned holiday music wafting through the air right now was something else… an odor or an image or a darkness that Percy could not quite catch, an energy that hovered just beyond the edge of normalcy and siphoned off of others. He could feel it, whatever it was, and he knew it was not ready to go away. He knew it was ready to create more complications.

Will and Tessa got out of the car that had just parked. Percy watched them, noting that their bond had strengthened in the short time they'd known each other. He smiled. Love during the Christmas season was very special.

He raised his arm and waved as Will approached the steps. "Will, my friend, it's been a while. How are you?"

Will smiled and hugged Percy. "Great to see you. Should be a good meeting, tonight, right?"

Percy nodded and spoke before Will could walk away. "I hate to impose, because I know how busy you are, but I need to talk with you, Will. It's very important." When Will hesitated and looked at Tessa, Percy rushed to finish what he needed to say. "I don't mind at all if Tessa is there; in fact, it would probably be better if she was. Truly, I wouldn't disturb you if I didn't feel this was critical."

"Does this have anything to do with Tessa?" Will asked, taking a combative posture.

Percy made a soothing gesture with his hands. "No, not directly. But it does impact you, so I think that would affect her." He looked at both of them standing in front of him. "I have the impression that if something serious is going on with one of you then the other would want to know, right?"

Will nodded. "Okay, let's talk after the meeting. Can you at least tell me what this is about? It's not really fair to leave me hanging, you know."

Percy hesitated before speaking, but he knew he had to be honest. "It's about Dahlia. I have some information I'd like to share with you."

Will's gaze was piercing. Finally, he let out a big sigh. "In that case why don't we go back to my house tonight. I have a feeling this could take a while."

Chapter Six

Will took his time lighting the fire in the fireplace. The house was cold lately, and despite turning the thermostat up a couple of degrees the chill in the air would not dispel. He couldn't help but wonder if the lack of warmth had something to do with Dahlia. *That's crazy. But I can't stop thinking there's a connection that I've missed.*

"Have you noticed that the house has been cold lately?" Tessa said, echoing Will's thoughts. "The apartment is like that, too. It feels like an Arctic blast has pushed its way in and taken root in these buildings."

"I think it's from the recent events that have happened here," Percy said from the couch. He and Tessa were seated, watching Will as he stepped back from the roaring blaze he'd just constructed. When Will sat in the wingback chair facing them, he said, "Let's talk. How do you know Dahlia?"

Percy sat very still for a moment. Will knew he was struggling with his thoughts, and he allowed Percy a moment to speak. "I have a newspaper article I'd like to show you." Reaching into a computer bag that he had carried in with him, Percy pulled out a stack of yellowed papers. "You need to be careful reading these, the newspaper is quite old and brittle."

Will leaned forward and looked at the banner on the newspaper. "The Richmond Dispatch... wait... 1926?"

When Percy nodded, Will reached out, picked up the paper, and scanned the front page. "Am I supposed to be reading the headline article?"

"No, the article below the fold. On the bottom of the first page."

Will flipped the paper over. The picture stared back at him, sending a jolt of electricity through his body. When Tessa came and stood next to him, he angled the paper so she could get a better look at it. "That's her, isn't it?" Tessa asked.

"It must be someone related to her," Will said. "Because it looks exactly like her."

"No, I'm sorry, but Tessa is correct. The picture on the front page is Dahlia," Percy said.

"It can't be. This paper is from 1926. Is the paper real?" Will said, turning it over and examining it to determine authenticity.

"The paper is real," Percy said. "And I'm sorry if I upset you, but I think it's time you knew the truth."

"She lived here, didn't she?" Tessa said. "It makes sense, what Will was saying about how he would see her sometimes but she wasn't really there. She died here, didn't she?"

***

Tessa didn't know why the men were so surprised when she said that. The article in front of her was very clear: *Woman*

Murdered At Farmhouse. Seriously, she'd have to be an idiot not to connect the dots on this.

But sometimes it took people a bit longer to believe what was right in front of them. Maybe her life experience opened her up to different concepts about reality, but she had no trouble whatsoever with the idea that things existed outside of the "normal" that most people lived with. Quickly scanning the article, the coldness that had seeped through her body seemed to intensify. Almost shivering, she looked up at Will.

"She didn't just die, she was murdered," Tessa said. "Here. At this house." Pointing at the article, Tessa continued to read. "It says that because they found so much blood in the front yard, plus the drag marks, they believe whoever did it killed her and stuffed her in the basement." Tessa looked up, tears swimming in her eyes. "They never found the husband, did they?"

Percy shook his head. "You are correct, they never found the husband. But—"

"Will, you've got to get her back," Tessa said. "Now."

Will's face was a blend of confusion and fear. "I don't know what you—"

"How did she leave?" Tessa asked, a note of impatience in her voice. "When you kicked Dahlia out of the house, which door did she walk out of?"

Will slumped against the back of the chair and let out a breath. "I don't know. I asked her to leave, then she was gone. I never actually saw her go out a door or anything. She was here, then she wasn't."

"Exactly," Tessa said. "She faded into wherever she went, but she's not here with us. I think you banished her."

"What are you talking about?" Will said, practically yelling. "This whole thing doesn't make any sense. She was some crazy chick who got on Facebook and pretended to be someone, then she showed up here—"

A sense of urgency gripped Tessa. If she had learned one thing in her life, one life-saving thing, this was it: always trust your instincts. And right now her instincts were screaming at her that they had to find a way to get Dahlia back, in this house, before it was too late.

Chapter Seven

Tessa's fear almost paralyzed her. Something very dark was coming, she could feel it. "Hurry, Will, call her back, before it's too late."

"What are you talking about?" Will said. "Before what's too late? You're safe here, calm down. Maybe you're right, but I can't just get on Facebook—"

"No, you don't do it on Facebook. You have to invite her in, or something like that. Or ask her to be here, I don't know," Tessa said. "Percy, how does this work?"

Percy nodded. "She's right. Dahlia is—was—the guardian spirit of this house. Her job was to protect the residents from any evil that might try to get in. When you told her she had to go, she had no choice but to leave. I do not believe she can come back unless you invite her in."

"You don't believe? Don't you know for sure?" Will asked.

Percy shook his head. "No. I've never dealt with this type of situation before."

"Who are you?" Will said. "You're not who you said you are."

"I am exactly who I said I am. Remember I told you I worked for a higher power?"

"You said you were a therapist."

Percy shrugged. "That's part of it. But I do a sort of consulting work here, and I try to help those I've been assigned to help. This particular assignment is somewhat different from anything I've ever done before."

The ticking of the clock blended with the sound of Tessa's labored breathing. They didn't have time for this conversation, action needed to happen now. A wave of dark dread descended on the house. *How can they not feel that? How can they stand there as if nothing were happening?*

"You need to do something," Tessa whispered, immobilized by her own emotions.

"I think we need to sit down and talk about this some more," Will said.

Tessa turned and walked to the front window, where the starless night lay stretched wide like a trap. Will kept talking. "I'm not saying I don't believe you, but we need to approach this in a rational way. Let's start with what we know, and then we can formulate a plan."

A humming started inside Tessa, as if her insides were made from taut violin strings. Her mouth was dry and her hands shook. *Can they hear it?* she wondered. *Do they know it's coming from me, that screeching sound?*

She knew without turning around that Will had sat in the chair again, but Percy remained standing. "Tessa, it's going to be okay," Will said.

"No, it's not," she answered. "You need to call her back right now. Stop waiting to talk, stop wondering what's going on, just call her. Now."

"Why?" Will said.

"Because he's here," she answered as a wave of headlights washed through the room.

***

Dahlia couldn't remember being born, but she decided it must have been very much like what was happening right now. Opening before her, a large whirlpool pulled her in with a gentle whooshing sound, and she hurtled her way through the tunnel-like structure toward the end. The sensation was not unpleasant, but she definitely had no control or ability to move. Gentle waves of energy pulsed over her and propelled her into the house she had come to love and consider home. The main difference was that this time nobody could see her.

Both Will and Percy stood as if frozen. Will had his hands in front of him in a placating gesture, clearly trying to calm whoever was in the house. "I don't think this is a very good idea. The police are on the way. And so is Dahlia."

Tessa was moving away from the window, inching toward the kitchen. Dahlia knew she was trying to be unobtrusive, but unfortunately the intruder was fixated on her.

The intruder laughed, an ugly sound that Dahlia knew well. "Nobody is on the way, kid. And don't worry, I'll make it painless for you and the old man."

"Leave them alone," Tessa said in a hoarse voice. "They didn't do anything. Will, where is she?"

The snarl was evident in the man's voice. "Nobody's coming to save you, sugar. And these guys have been harboring stolen property. I think that constitutes a crime."

"She's not property," Will yelled, lunging at the man. His punch was easily blocked by the man, who then raised a large metal pipe over his head and slammed it onto Will. Will crumpled into a heap on the ground. He then turned and slammed the same pipe into Percy's center. The pipe made a thudding sound when it connected, and Percy collapsed without a whimper.

"Easier than shooting, don't you think, sugar?"

Tessa stood next to the hutch that held an array of fine china and crystal. Dahlia pushed aside the fear that threatened to consume her. *So, he's back. This is what I've been waiting for.*

"Why aren't you in jail?" Tessa said.

"Because you are mine," the man said. "Because lawyers and judges and anybody in the world can be bought, and after that I get to come back and finish my business. Let's go." He made an impatient gesture. "If you won't come with me, I'll just kill you. I don't want to leave any loose ends, but I think I've spent enough time on you."

Dahlia drifted over to where Tessa stood, touching her lightly on the shoulder so that the woman would know she was not alone. *She is very sensitive, and I'm sure she felt that.* When Tessa straightened a little taller, Dahlia knew she was right. Tessa had felt her presence.

Dahlia continued to push on Tessa, edging her back toward the window. *Because I've waited all these years for this, to defend others from this exact evil.*

The man turned slightly, mocking Tessa. "What the hell do you think you're doing, getting ready to jump out the window?"

Almost... almost...

"She's only doing what I asked," Dahlia said, forcing herself to appear. A multitude of emotions crossed the man's face: confusion, fear, and finally, anger.

"Hello, Charles," Dahlia said as she drifted up toward the ceiling. "I can't say it's good to see you again, but this time I'm not going to let you get away with killing another innocent woman."

"What the hell—" Charles advanced toward Dahlia, fury in his movements. "What kind of trick is this? Do I know you—wait, yes, I—"

"You bet," Dahlia said as she shoved the hutch with all her might. Tessa hopped a little more out of the way as the heavy oak piece of furniture crashed down upon Charles. The noise of the falling piece and breaking glass resounded through the room. Dahlia grinned at Tessa. "And that, my dear, is how we take care of bad guys. Are you okay?"

Chapter Eight

Snow fell gently through the night, obscuring any ugliness that marred the landscape. Percy knocked on the door and waited, hoping that Tessa and Will liked carrot cake. It was all he could find on such short notice.

Tessa laughed when she opened the door and saw what Percy was holding. "Come in, please," she said. "It's kind of cold out there."

"That usually happens around this time of year. Merry Christmas!"

"Is that Percy?" Will hollered from the kitchen.

"Yes," Tessa laughed. "And he made us a carrot cake to go with our dinner."

"I wish I could taste it."

"Dahlia!" Percy said. "It's so wonderful to see you again."

"You mean now that I'm not pushing large pieces of furniture onto bad people?" Dahlia smiled as she said this, but Percy knew she held a hint of remorse at having to hurt another. Even if it was the man who had hurt her so long ago.

"Are you feeling okay?" he asked.

Dahlia glanced at Will, who had emerged from the kitchen, and Tessa, who was smiling at her. "I am wonderful. I am here in this beautiful home, with these amazing people. I have finally faced the man that killed me—"

"This still doesn't make any sense to me," Will said. "How could that guy be the one who killed you in 1926?"

"Reincarnation," Tessa said, nudging him with her elbow. "I've explained all this to you."

"But it still doesn't explain how she knew it was the same guy. It's not like they looked the same or anything," Will said.

"I recognized his true self," Dahlia said. "His spirit was right there for me to see it."

Percy crossed the room and handed the cake to Will. "I'm just glad everything worked out. And I assume that now that you are aware of Dahlia you will allow her to remain?"

Will nodded. "Of course. Since everything happened... my life, it's not the same. I don't think it ever will be. But Dahlia has spent so much time taking care of..." Percy waited, knowing that Will was overwhelmed with emotion. "She can stay, but she knows the rules." He leveled a look at her.

Dahlia put one hand on her hip and held up a finger. "First, no going in Will's room." She held up a second finger. "And no going in the bathroom." Then she held up a third finger. "And no scaring the guests. Easy peasy, I can do this."

Percy smiled, marveling again at how things had worked out. "And Tessa, how is your apartment?"

"Much better," Tessa said. "Especially now that Dahlia comes to visit. We like to play card games and talk."

Percy raised his eyebrows. "Card games?"

Will called over his shoulder as he walked back into the kitchen. "It's not the card games I'm worried about, it's the talking."

Percy smiled. The dining room table had already been set, and the dishes and glasses sparkled. "I thought you broke everything…"

"We did," Tessa said. "But Will had an entire attic full of stuff that had belonged to his grandmother. It was kind of fun going through it all and pulling out things we could use for our Christmas dinner. Are you hungry?"

Percy didn't tell her that no, he wasn't hungry. Because of what he was, he never got hungry. But he could sit and eat with them, sharing a meal and the warmth of Christmas. They probably had more questions, and he was ready to provide answers. They were good people who had faced darkness and won. Because of that, he was fairly certain this was one Christmas they would always remember.

CHRISTMAS

VAMPIRE BUNNY

JM JOHANSEN

Chapter One

Deltaville, Virginia is famous as the boat building capital of the Chesapeake Bay. It became my home in 2003 when I moved into a small cottage on Lovers Lane (yes, there is a Lovers Lane). Three weeks later Hurricane Isabel hit. It was my first hurricane and my first experience with power outages. Fourteen days of power outages. I learned what a generator was, how to cook on a Coleman stove, and I got to know my neighbors. They took care of me, made sure I was okay, and made me feel safe.

I am a "come here". That means I came here from somewhere else, as opposed to a "born here" who was, well, born here. Of course, I have met people who moved to Deltaville when they were two years old, are now eighty, and are still considered a "come here". Not that it matters—the Deltavillians are my fellow citizens, and in a pinch they don't care where you came from.

Deltaville is my home now. We are bordered by the Rappahannock River to the North, the Piankatank River to the south, and the Chesapeake Bay to the east. It's a quiet place to about 1,000 full time residents. However, I know it has its secrets. Some lie on the bottom of the rivers surrounding the village. Some live on in a rabbit cage buried in a backyard.

It was my first Christmas in Deltaville. I was far from home, had made a few friends, but still felt somewhat isolated. I had thought about Christmas, decided not to put up a tree and decorate, then changed my mind. *What have I got to be so bah-hum-bug about? After all, I made the decision to come here, so I have no one else to blame.*

My neighbor on the left was a "born here" who kept a large, floppy-eared rabbit in a cage in her fenced backyard. She was not very friendly, and since I was a Yankee, she didn't have too much to say to me. But she had strong opinions, and she let me know there she had no use for anyone who didn't celebrate Christmas.

"Aren't you gonna put up decorations? You know, the hayride come right by our houses and goes down to the public dock for the Jackson Creek boat tours. You don't wanna be the only house without no decorations."

"I really don't feel like it this year. Isabel sapped all my energy, and I'm not certain I could even find my decorations at this point."

She had a puzzled look on her face, so I continued. "See, when the hurricane came a lot of my things were ruined and everything else is in storage. I haven't gotten to it yet."

"I see." She turned and went back into her house.

The next morning when I returned from my shift at the hospital, there were two large boxes of Christmas ornaments and a small, freshly cut tree on my screened-in porch. I went over to thank her, but no one was home, so I left a note.

My neighbor on the other side was a "come here". She was a different story. Very friendly, very helpful, and someone I could rely on to let my dog out if I was held over at the hospital. She owned a chocolate lab who loved to play with my Border Collie. But Hershey—as the chocolate lab was called—also loved to dig under the fence and knock the rabbit from his perch. I think the lab wanted to play; the rabbit's owner didn't see it that way.

This went on for months—my neighbor on the left going off to work, the dog on the right digging under the fence and knocking the rabbit to the ground. Fussing, fighting, and finally a visit from the sheriff's deputy and his accomplice, the animal control officer. "Next time we're takin' the dog and youth-a-nizing him," the animal control officer proclaimed.

"Where's McGruff?" I asked.

"You mean the dog, McGruff?" the deputy asked.

"Yes. I thought maybe he could explain to Hershey why it's not nice—that rabbits aren't a chew toy. He speaks his language and it might help to talk with a peer. You know, take a bite outta crime."

They didn't think I was funny.

After that, the neighbors to the right built a fence. She was terrified at the thought of losing her lab, so she kept him locked up in their newly secured yard. Peace and tranquility returned to our little lane in Deltaville. Hershey (the lab) and Fluffy (the rabbit) remained in their proper places.

Until one Monday morning—the day before Christmas.

I was coming home from my shift at the hospital, eleven p.m. to seven a.m. It was freezing cold. My plan was to hurry to the back door, let the dog out, and warm up with some hot tea. My neighbor on the left had gone to work.

As I pulled into the driveway that separated our two houses I noticed Hershey coming out from under the "come here" neighbor's fence. He had Fluffy in his mouth. Both were covered with mud and the rabbit was not moving.

I went next door and got my neighbor (who became hysterical at the site of the dead rabbit). "They're going to kill Hersey! What am I going to do?" she screamed.

"I have a plan," I said. "You take Hershey home, get him cleaned up and let me tend to the rabbit."

I took the bunny into the house, plopped his lifeless body into the kitchen sink and got the shampoo out of the bathroom. I washed him, then took my hair dryer and blew him dry. He looked great, and fortunately had no bite marks from his ill-fated encounter with Hershey.

My neighbor met me outside. "What's your plan?" she asked.

"My plan is to put the rabbit back in his hutch and when you-know-who comes home, there he will be—in his hutch. She'll assume he died of natural causes and all will be well once again."

We went next door, opened the gate and placed the hutch in its proper upright position. I filled the rabbit's dishes with the food that had spilled out on the ground, put water in the bowl, and closed the door to the hutch. We left the back yard. "Keep Hershey locked up," I told my neighbor and new-found "I-owe-you-for-the-rest-of-my-life" friend. "Merry Christmas," I said as I went back into the house.

I cleaned up the kitchen and went to bed. I had to be at work at eleven p.m. and needed some sleep if I was going to be coherent. I got up at around five-thirty p.m. just in time to see the rabbit owner come home from work. I decided to hang around and watch from the kitchen window.

She opened the gate, started toward the back door, stopped, and began screaming, "Fluffy! Fluffy!" I put my coat on and walked from my back deck across the yard and through her open gate.

"What happened?" I asked.

"Fluffy, fluffy," she yelled. "Fluff!"

I walked over to the cage, looked in, and said, "Oh, my goodness—I am so sorry. Poor Fluffy seems to be el morte!"

"I don't know who el morte is, but Fluffy is dead. Dead!" She seemed on the verge of hysteria.

"I am so sorry." By now the entire neighborhood was in the back yard. My neighbor across the street, who was extremely hard of hearing, asked if he needed to call the rescue squad, thinking someone was ill. There Fluffy was, warm as toast with his little hutch heater running full tilt.

"No," I told him. "The rabbit has died."

"Well the rescue squad doesn't do animals," he said. "You 'come heres' are just too used to city living."

"Yes, well anyway, let's get my neighbor here calmed down." I pulled a chair over for her so she could sit down before she fell down.

"You don't understand," she kept saying over and over. "You just don't understand!"

Now, I understand attachment to pets—even rabbits—but not to the extent this poor soul was exhibiting. She was sobbing, shaking, screaming Fluffy's name over and over.

Finally, she stopped, looked up, and said "You don't understand. This morning, before I left for work, I came out to feed Fluffy."

"I do understand," I said.

"No, let me finish! He wasn't moving. He died sometime last night, I guess. So I buried him before I left for work. Took me a while, because the ground was kinda hard and I had to use the pickax to loosen up the soil." She pointed to the hole on the left side of the yard. "And now he's back in his cage like nothing happened."

I looked at my watch. "Oops, late for work!" I said as I made a hasty exit. All of the other neighbors disbanded quickly, leaving my neighbor to tend to resurrection rabbit.

The rabbit's owner never figured it out. She did tell me she thought the house was haunted, started talking about vampires, a zombie apocalypse, and other things.

I certainly wasn't going to tell her the whole story…for Hershey's sake. I didn't want to see the poor dog "youth-a-nized".

She moved the next year.

Oh—and the rabbit? I think he's either buried in his cage under the tree in her back yard (the one she hung garlic on all the time) or he's lying on the bottom of the river.

Either way, the Christmas Bunny is resting comfortably…somewhere.

LUCKY CHRISTMAS

NARIELLE LIVING

Chapter One

I t was one thirty a.m., well past the time to go home. Kylie took a deep breath and leaned over to put her cell phone back in her bag. The remaining convenience store coffee she was holding had grown cold and a headache was forming behind her eyes from the strain of the evening. The only problem was now that it was time to go, she had to tell him. She still had not been able to form the words that needed to be said.

The radio in the car crackled to life. Kylie wondered how anyone could possibly understand the dispatchers. To her, it sounded like nothing but static with lots of incoherent words. Glancing at Nick sitting in the driver's seat, her heart sank. She could tell from the look on his face, not to mention the way he peeled out of the parking lot, she was not going home yet.

"What's going on?" Maybe she didn't want to know.

"Shots fired." Kylie waited for him to elaborate, knowing he wouldn't. Unfailingly polite and not bad to look at, Nick was definitely a man of few words. Or maybe he just didn't want to talk to her.

Shrinking into her seat, she tried not to think of what that phrase meant. Despite the clean, suburban persona of Yorktown, images of gangsters with guns floated through her head. *That kind of thing doesn't happen here, does it?* Unlikely as the possibility was, she didn't want to die from a gunshot wound. *And I don't want to die before Christmas.*

After flipping the siren on, Nick pulled out a cell phone and began barking rapid fire questions to the person on the other end. Removing his remaining hand from the steering wheel, he used his right knee to steer the car as he leaned forward to punch an address into the GPS attached to the windshield. Wherever they were going, it was faster to get there by taking the highway. Watching the speedometer needle climb to ninety, Kylie closed her eyes and held tight to her paper coffee cup. *Please, let there be no ice on the highway... please...*

Kylie dared to open her eyes only when the car slowed. They had entered an industrial area, a part of town she didn't even know existed. Maybe her timing sucked, but if they were going to get shot, she wanted him to know.

"Nick, I have to tell you something."

"C'mon, I know you're here somewhere... they always try to hide, but this time I'm going to catch the little—gotcha!" Slamming on the brakes, he threw the police car into park and opened his door. Shooting a stern look over his shoulder, Nick barked one command. "Stay in the car."

That's pretty much when it all fell apart.

***

Nick could barely feel the ice pack he held on the growing lump on his head. Anger always made him hot, so it was a wonder the ice wasn't immediately turning into water. He shifted on the plastic chair, trying to get comfortable. He had a feeling the captain had ordered these chairs specifically to keep his men off balance.

At the moment, the captain was sitting across from him, leaning forward with his hands on his desk. At least his face wasn't red, and he was only glaring a little. Nick knew when the captain's face got red he was in real trouble.

"Well, deputy, can you tell me what happened out there last night?"

"Yes, sir. I was doing a ride along with a civilian—"

"Kylie," the captain said. "The woman assigned to you."

"Yes sir, Kylie. At the end of my shift I got a call for shots fired in the upper part of the county. I radioed in and responded. When we got there, I told her to stay in the car. I circled around to try to find the perpetrator, and the next thing I know the officer needs help alarm went off and then deputies from all over swarmed in."

The captain looked stern, but Nick wondered if he was really angry. Usually officers who worked with the captain always knew when they were in trouble by the look on his face. Today, though, annoyance did not reach his eyes. "Did you tell her not to touch that particular button in the vehicle?"

"I told her, I swear I told her, but she must not have been listening, because for some reason she decided to push the red button."

The captain cleared his throat. "I believe she said that she thought you were in danger, deputy."

Nick was confused. How could she have thought he was in any kind of danger? As soon as he realized he had stumbled into a group of residents setting off fireworks, he issued a warning and left. Everybody had been very polite to him. It wasn't until later that morning he learned he had walked into the middle of an undercover operation, but that had not put him in any danger. It had, however, exposed him to ridicule from the detectives he worked with.

The captain, looking stern again, interrupted Nick's thoughts. "Why doesn't your siren work anymore?"

Nick wasn't sure how to answer. He didn't want to get Kylie in trouble, but he wasn't going to take the heat for this one. Trying to sidestep the issue, he said, "I think some coffee might have gotten spilled in the car, sir."

"Coffee."

"Yes, sir."

"And tell me one more thing, deputy."

Nick would answer this question and maybe hopefully get to go home. He was exhausted, and not only from lack of sleep. That Kylie woman had a way of wearing him out.

"Sir?"

"How did you get a black eye last night?"

Nick swallowed. He had been expecting this and knew he had to answer as truthfully as possible. Hopefully nobody else would find out about this. He didn't want his co-workers to know what had happened.

"I walked into a door, sir. Kylie opened the car door as I was walking over to the car, and it caught me on the side of the head, near my eye."

This time the captain could not stop the grin that spread across his face. "That'll be all, deputy. You better keep that ice pack on your head. And you should go out in the hall and talk to Kylie, she's waiting for you."

Nick couldn't stop the groan that escaped. "What does she want?"

The captain stopped smiling and looked at Nick with something akin to concern. "I think you should give her a chance, she's got something interesting to tell you." Staring for another moment, he added, "I didn't notice it before, but you have the same eyes."

Nick had no idea what the captain was talking about. All he wanted was to get home and sleep. The late night shifts left him exhausted. Saying goodbye, he strode into the hallway to find Kylie sitting in a chair, waiting for him. Without censoring himself, he cut into her. "What the hell were you thinking?"

"You shouldn't clench your jaw like that; it'll give you a headache."

Nick suppressed his urge to yell, realizing it wouldn't do any good. The woman had seemed nice enough at the beginning of the night, but she was quickly proving herself to be the biggest pain in the you-know-what he had ever met. There was a reason most of the deputies didn't like having civilians riding in their cars, but once in a while it had to be done. Twice yearly the department taught a class called the Citizen's Academy, where every week students learned about all facets of law enforcement. Part of the class included riding with a deputy to get a better perspective of the job. For some reason, this woman, Kylie what's-her-name, whom he had never met or seen or even knew existed, had requested him specifically for her ride along.

Lucky him. Maybe this was his early Christmas present.

Rubbing a hand over a day's worth of stubble, Nick took a deep breath. "Okay, I'll ask this once, as nicely as I can. What was the one thing I told you not to do?"

Kylie hung her head, allowing her long auburn hair to cover her face. She didn't say anything for a moment.

Nick cupped his hand around his ear. "I'm sorry, I can't hear you. I know you know the answer to this: the one thing you were not supposed to do…"

She didn't look up. "Don't touch the button," she mumbled.

"Right," he answered in a falsely bright voice. "Don't touch the button. And what did you do?"

Snapping her head up, she glared at him for the first time. "I—"

"Touched the button," he finished for her.

"I thought you were—"

Pointing his finger in her face, he spoke over her. "Not only did you set off an alarm that caused every law enforcement agent in three counties to high tail it over to us, you also managed to disable the siren on the vehicle as well as give me a black eye. I had to explain all that to my captain just now."

They glared at each other for a moment until Kylie looked away. She spoke with an obvious effort. "I was trying to help. I thought those guys were going to attack you, how was I supposed to know they were setting off fireworks? And it wasn't my fault the coffee spilled on the console. Those things shouldn't be able to short out as easy as that, you know. Someone should look into upgrading the equipment."

Nick sighed, running his hand through his already tousled dark hair. He knew she hadn't meant any harm, but what was it they said about the road to hell? "Yeah, and I know you didn't mean to whack me in the face with the car door, it just happened, right?"

"You don't have to be so mean to me."

As her eyes filled with tears Nick purposely hardened his heart. She was like a walking Hallmark movie, an obnoxious Christmas one. It was obvious she wanted something from him, but he wasn't about to let her use histrionics to get it. Towering over her, knowing she was uncomfortable in that stupid plastic chair, he used a deliberately neutral voice. "So, what was it you wanted to tell me?"

For the second time that morning, Kylie glared at him. "You know what? I don't think I want to talk to you right now. You haven't been very nice to me, and all I was trying to do was help. I think I'll let your captain tell you all about it."

Nick straightened. He really did not have time for this. "He told me to talk to you, and he said we have the same eyes. I'm only going to ask you one more time. What's going on?"

Kylie stood, knocking her chair over in the process. "We're here because I know what I did last night I probably shouldn't have done, and I'm sorry there was such a fuss over one little button. I had to explain that to them so *you* wouldn't get into trouble. But in the process of explaining myself, I also told your captain some other things."

"What kind of things?" Nick said. *Was she always this evasive? Why couldn't she just answer a simple damn question?*

"Things about our father."

Realization was slow for Nick. Her words jostled around in his head, not really making sense. It took him a full minute to process what she said, and during that time numbness crawled through him.

"What do you mean, our father? Exactly who are you talking about?" Because there was no way this bubbly, energetic woman had a father anything like his.

She straightened her shoulders and wiped away her tears. "Your captain has my phone number if you decide to contact me."

Spinning to leave, she tripped on the heel of her boot. Nick grabbed her arm to stop her fall. *This girl is going to hurt herself one of these days.* He couldn't help but wonder at the angry look she shot him as she wrenched her arm away. It wasn't his fault she created so much havoc wherever she went.

***

December in Virginia was usually cold, but that morning it cut through Kylie more than usual. She shivered, pulled her coat closer around her, and hurried to her car. Things had not gone the way she'd expected. Nick was mean. None of what happened was her fault. Trying to protect someone should be applauded, not condemned.

She stopped at the door to her car, patting her pockets. *Where did I put my keys? Did I lose them?* She dug through her purse, finally finding them. Shivering, freezing cold, she grabbed the keys from the bottom of her bag and yanked them out, only to have them fly out of her hands and skitter under the car.

This keeps getting better. Get the darn keys, get in your car, go home, and go to bed. Everything will go away then. She bent and could see them just within her reach. On her hands and knees now, she stretched her arm toward the keys. Feet appeared on the other side of her vehicle. *This does not look good.* Her butt was in the air and her face was smashed against the underside of the car door as she tried to reach the keys. She couldn't help that she heard the conversation happening, or that they didn't realize she was right there.

"Glad it wasn't more serious," the first voice said. "But I heard he got it pretty good in the face."

Kylie cringed, knowing who they were talking about.

"Yeah, but at least putting that ice pack on his injury will give him something to focus on over the holidays," a second voice said.

"Don't be mean. I like him, he's just a loner, that's all."

"He works all the time," the second voice said. Kylie had dropped down to her stomach and could see two pairs of feet standing on the other side of her car. The voice continued. "I know he doesn't have any family, but it's not right that he's always here."

"Maybe he likes it that way," the first voice said.

Yeah, maybe he likes it that way. But Kylie knew better.

"I've got to go, the wife is expecting me to watch the kids while she finishes Christmas shopping."

"Good luck with that. This time of year they are all worked up."

"Yeah. Merry Christmas!"

Kylie stayed on the ground, waiting for them to go away. When the sound of the departing cars finally faded, she got up, unlocked her door, and climbed into her driver's seat. Leaning back, she closed her eyes and tried to hold back tears. That conversation changed everything. She knew what she had to do now, but ultimately it would be up to Nick. She couldn't force him into anything, but she sure could try.

Chapter Two

Nick was grateful for the cover of the night. With the combination of clouds and new moon it was easy to blend with the darkness. The crisp, cold air soothed his tangled nerves. Standing by the tree in the front yard, he could easily see into the front living room where the family had gathered.

They looked happy enough, but his father's words echoed through his mind. "Just cuz they're smilin' don't mean they're happy. Everybody's after something, boy." As if the ghost were by his side, Nick could practically hear him. "What do you want from these people, anyway? More heartache? Stupid kid."

Bitterness rose in his throat as he watched Kylie hug a woman of about sixty, presumably her mother. Memories of his own mother's less than maternal slaps and punches reminded him that not everyone was as fortunate as Kylie. Not everyone got the good home. *Merry freakin' Christmas. I'll bet it's just perfect in there.*

Lost in his thoughts, Nick was startled by the sound of the front door opening. "Nick, are you out there?"

How did she know? She must be some kind of witch. He hesitated, then sighed and stepped forward. He'd better talk to her before she did something calamitous and caused a scene.

"I'm here."

Unbelievably, she smiled at him, radiant. "I knew you'd come."

"How did you know I was already here?"

She gave a half shrug, looking somewhat embarrassed. "You're a cop—I mean, deputy. I figured you'd want to scope the place out before you came in to meet us. Besides, it's Christmas. We're family. It all makes sense."

Actually it didn't, but he wasn't going to argue that point with her. He was defiant. "Just because you left me a message didn't mean I would come. I never called you back to let you know I would be here."

Kylie gazed at him thoughtfully. "Of course you would be here. You're my big brother, aren't you?"

A wave of guilt washed through him. "Half brother," Nick corrected.

Kylie waved a hand at him. "Half, schmalf, who cares how much it is. The point is, I always figured that if I had a brother he would be a great friend and protect me and be lots of fun to hang out with. He could walk me to school and beat up boys that tried to date me. I used to think about that when I was a girl."

Nick was puzzled. "I thought you just found out about me."

"I did. Mom only told me last month she had heard that my, I mean our, father had another child. It's been a long time since they've seen each other, you know."

Nick nodded. "Since the day you were born, right?"

Kylie sucked in her breath. "Did you know about me?"

"No, but I knew about our father." He was not the nicest human being, but he was all Nick had growing up. A half-memory floated by of another Christmas when he was about seven years old. Nick had woken up Christmas morning knowing that what he'd really wanted was not going to be under the tree. A sober father, a bigger family. Those things were just not going to happen in his little world. As he got older, he'd heard the rumors about the other family, the whispers about his father. If he was to be honest with himself, which he probably should right about now, he'd always known a day like this would come.

She looked off into the distance. "I wish we had grown up together, but I can't change that. I would like for you to get to know us, though. You've got nieces and a nephew, and my mother really wants to meet you."

Nick's throat closed, surprising him. Why should he care if some woman wanted to meet him? *Because she's the mother you never knew.* He cleared his throat before speaking. "I'm not very good at family stuff, you know."

"You don't have to be good at family stuff, you just have to care."

Nick was frustrated. It was obvious that Kylie didn't understand where he had come from, what his family life was like growing up. She was one of the lucky kids who got tucked in at night and had bedtime stories read to her. He was lucky just to have a roof over his head. At least that's what his old man told him.

"Mom told me all about him." Kylie's voice was soft in the night. This time it was Nick's turn to look into the darkness.

"Yeah, well, I'm sure it was the same old story, his father was probably a jerk to him, too."

"Is that why you don't have any of your own kids?"

His own laugh sounded harsh in his ears. "No, I've just never really met the right woman. But you're probably right, I don't think I'm exactly father material."

Kylie shook her head. "That's not what I meant and you know it. Come on, you're just trying to delay all this. Come in the house and meet everyone. For heaven's sake, it's Christmas. Have a little holiday spirit."

Nick looked into the house again, which was more of a home than he'd ever known. The Christmas tree lights were flashing, and people were moving back and forth, talking and laughing. Maybe it would be okay to go in and meet them all, just this once. He looked down at Kylie, bouncing on the balls of her feet, excited for him to be there, and sighed.

"Fine, let's go in. But do me a favor, okay?"

Kylie smiled. "Sure, brother, what is it?"

He knew he was asking the impossible, but he had to try. "Can you try to not get us into any more trouble for a while?"

Kylie's smile faded as doubt crossed her face. "I don't mean for bad stuff to happen..."

"It just does," he finished for her. "For my sake, try. It will make my job as your big brother a whole lot easier." He smiled at her to try to take the sting out of the words, but he was serious. That girl knew how to create havoc wherever she went. "All right, I'm ready." He knew his life had changed the moment Kylie found him, and he knew her persistence would not allow him to be left alone. Ready or not, he was about to get a new family.

Walking behind her, Nick was so lost in thought he didn't realize Kylie had stopped walking until it was almost too late. Trying not to plow into her, he lurched backward, lost his balance and fell. Unaware that he had fallen, Kylie turned and said, "Oh, there's one more thing I wanted to tell you."

Nick looked up from the ground. "What?"

"What are you doing on the ground?"

Rising, he slowly brushed himself off. "Nothing. What did you want to tell me?"

"I got a new job!"

Nick froze, the hairs on the back of his neck tingling. He had that feeling he always got right before something big happened, usually something that involved people getting shot or car doors slamming into his face.

He almost didn't want to ask. "What's the job?"

The glow on her face made his heart sink even further. "I got a job with the sheriff's department. I'm going to be the public relations person. Isn't that great? We're going to be working together!"

Nick smiled weakly. It was the best he could do, considering the effect he knew she would have on the department.

"Great," he echoed. "Isn't that... lucky. For you, I mean."

"Nick, I just know it's going to be a wonderful New Year!"

ABOUT THE BAY SISTERS

JULIE LEVERENZ

Julie Leverenz, writer and photographer, has won Firsts in the Virginia Writers Club Golden Nib contest (nonfiction), VWC Summer Shorts (fiction) and the York County Library Juried Literary Competition (poetry). Her essays and photos have appeared in the **Virginia Gazette** and the **Daily Press**. Julie also contributed a short story and a poem to the Chesapeake Bay Writers Anthology, **Harboring Secrets**. A New Jersey native, Julie earned degrees at Dickinson College and the College of William and Mary, where she founded the Women in Business Program. Julie lives in Virginia with her husband and a multi-talented cat. More information can be found at www.julieleverenz.com.

NARIELLE LIVING

Narielle Living is a freelance writer and editor based out of the tidewater area of Virginia. She is a regular contributor for the Williamsburg magazine *Next Door Neighbors*, and has written hundreds of do-it-yourself articles for online magazines. She is the author of the mysteries *Signs of the South, Revenge of the Past*, and *Madness in Brewster Square*, and co-authored *Chesapeake Bay Karma—The Amulet*. Her fiction also appears in the anthologies *Chesapeake Bay Christmas Volume I, Chesapeake Bay Christmas Volume II, Chesapeake Bay Christmas Volume III*, and *Harboring*

Secrets. She edits both fiction and non-fiction, and loves helping other writers achieve their goals. A former massage therapist and healing arts educator, she studied Philosophy and Religion at Albertus Magnus College in New Haven, CT. Narielle is currently working on a true crime novel based on events in Gloucester County in 2011. For information about her books or workshops, visit www.narielleliving.com.

JM JOHANSEN

JM (Jeanne) Johansen is an Acquisitions Director for *High Tide Publications, Inc.* She teaches classes for Fire Bellied Frog, a national group formed to help writers with the mechanics of writing. She is the author of *27 Minutes*, co-author of *Chesapeake Bay Karma – The*

Amulet, and has published numerous articles for the magazine Chesapeake Style. Her fiction won second place in the Virginia Writers Club Golden Nib contest. Her work has also appeared in anthologies *Chesapeake Bay Christmas Volume I*, *Chesapeake Bay Christmas Volume II*, *Chesapeake Bay Christmas Volume III*, and *Harboring Secrets*. A California girl, she earned degrees at The University of San Francisco and Columbia State University. Jeanne is passionate about helping authors achieve publication of their work. Jeanne lives in Virginia with her husband, two dogs, and a vampire cat. More information: www.JeanneJohansen.com